Anna's Passion

Nick Taddeo

Foremost Press
Cedarburg, Wisconsin

Also by Nick Taddeo

August in the Mind
Tinnemaha Creek
Night Wine

Nick Taddeo
Pasadena, California

Published by Foremost Press
www.foremostpress.com

ISBN-10: 1-936154-68-4
ISBN-13: 978-1-936154-68-5

To Anastasia, my mother,
whose strength of character
and unyielding determination,
infuses Anna of the novel

CHAPTER 1

A single grape dangling on the shoot of a mature vine holds all the promise of a child about to take a first step into the unknown. That was Anastasia in her youth: excited, unknowing, bright, unschooled, yet longing to begin her life in a profession governed by nature's unfathomable whims.

Anna's greatest fortune, some might say misfortune, was that she was born into a winemaking family. The fermented elixir became a vital part of her existence since she was old enough to take a sip. Though the dark-haired, fiery-tempered young woman felt the success of the winery she was operating might be in danger, could even collapse at any time, she remained committed to the profession she loved and especially to the pursuit of making the finest wine in all of Napa Valley.

Friends of hers with similar opportunities to remain in the wine business chose to seek employment in occupations from which they could expect a regular salary. Anna would never under any circumstances consider attempting some other activity with her life. By her own choice, beyond gaining hands-on experience working in the vineyards alongside the seasonal laborers and inside her family's and the neighbors' wineries, she went on to study enology at the University of Davis—all with an unwavering devotion to the art of making wine.

However, appreciation of her inheritance was not on her mind at the moment. She believed her father was the primary cause for her current distress. Joseph Pugliesi, an easygoing man, who technically still owned the *Immelhoff Winery*, had gotten into deep financial trouble, and according to Anna was also stifling any potential for growth with their estate wines. His eighty-plus acres were situated between St. Helena and Calistoga with the Mayacamas lifting the western reaches of the land allowing for good drainage.

Working a few barrels away from Anna was Federica, a tall, pretty cellar master, who would have been at home on a fashion runway, but today wore high rubber boots over long slim legs. Dressed in worker's jeans, a plaid shirt and a small scarf wrapped tightly around her light brunette hair, she observed while Anna drew a portion of wine from an aging barrel into a glass tube. Federica said nothing but clearly sensed the tension from the young woman who any moment might erupt into an emotional fury.

Anastasia squirted about half of the purple liquid from the wine thief into a glass. She swirled it around, sipped a little and angrily spit it out. "Damn it! He's doing it again. I told that man not to use the microfilter."

Federica, two years older than Anna and somewhat hesitant to speak out, not because she was a shy person but because she learned to be cautious around Anastasia, set down the pressure-steam hose she was using and walked over to where her sister was working between rows of oak barrels stored in one of the three cool tunnels of their *Immelhoff Winery.*

"Anna, that man you are talking about is our father. Why do you always refer to him in the third person?"

"It's simple. I want to remove him as far as I can. He's too old to be in the wine business."

"Fifty-eight is not old."

"It is when his ideas are stalemated in the last century."

"That's just not fair. The Pugliesis have been making good wine since our great grandfather started this winery. Dad is simply continuing the tradition."

"Listen to you, Federica; sounds as though you're getting brave enough to speak your mind. I like that. Wish you'd do it more often."

"Well, maybe I don't know as much about winemaking as you. I admit it."

"Don't back off. You were just getting somewhere."

"No, Anna, you are powerful like the Mayacamas up there that water our vines. I'm just one of the shoots we trim off every year to keep the rest of the vine strong."

"Enough of that! One thing I would like to ask you. Maybe I could get you to go along with me on this."

"What is that?" Federica asked.

"Why do we still use the name *Immelhoff Winery*? A name like that doesn't catch anyone's attention. It sounds so dated, carries no romance, no allure. It makes me cringe every time I hear it."

"I'm sure you know the story. Our great grandfather Amerigo worked for Kurt Immelhoff, the man who originally owned this property and named the winery after himself."

"Of course I know the story. I'm wondering why we still hang onto the label. Immelhoff couldn't make a decent bottle of wine himself. That's why he hired the original Pugliesi to bail him out. Our relatives have since developed this winery, added the Emma Mae Vineyard, kept it all operating through storms, Prohibition and pestilence. By now, we should have the right to rename it if we want."

"I suppose so, but what would we call it? Pugliesi doesn't exactly light up much of an image either."

"No. I'll have to think about that. Perhaps it will come out of something we do or experience here," she said.

Anna first reflected on how she had been thrown into the mix by birth, almost as though the wine was coursing through her blood. That got her nowhere. She kicked around a few names. Nothing grabbed her so she let that lie fallow for a while.

She stopped mulling over those thoughts and said to her sister, "We were talking about our father. Taste this wine. It reminds me of him." Anastasia grimaced from the lack of aftertaste from the wine she had just sampled. "This stuff he insisted on blending last season has no flavor, no aroma. It's just flat and boring. If he has to meddle, he should stay with the plastic pink designer stuff he manages to sell and not use our winery's name at all, or better yet get himself out of this business altogether."

"But he wants to make good wines as much as you do."

"There are new techniques he's never heard about and won't even listen to."

"Anna, I know you. You're not as callous as you sound. Besides Dad is not a hardhead. He would listen to you, if you ever gave him a chance."

"Dad should have had a son. Since he didn't, I'm the one who has to take charge." She grabbed a mallet and slammed a wooden plug into the bunghole from which she had extracted the sample of wine. "Look at this. I told him to use silicone plugs. These wooden stoppers won't keep out the bacteria. Wine has been spoiled for centuries because of outdated methods. And these barrels! They're not made from split wood. These staves were cut with a saw. Even a traditionalist, as he thinks he is, should know better. Can't he do anything right?"

Federica returned to the pressure-steam hose she had been using to clean out the insides of the barrels. That had to be done so the tannins and bacteria from the previous usage wouldn't influence the new vintage.

"Don't bother with that," Anna instructed. "I don't intend to use those barrels."

"Why not? Dad loves these barrels. They've been used for some of our best wines."

"That's the point: used and reused. The pores in the wood are so clogged up, there's no chance for proper oxidation or oak flavor to influence the wine."

"I can shave the insides. That usually adds a season or two to their usage."

"You'd have to take the barrels apart and rebuild them afterwards, not worth the effort."

"I could just add wood chips like they're doing in some wineries to get fresh oak flavor."

"Not with my wine! Federica, why don't you take the rest of the day off? I want to work alone for a while."

Federica certainly didn't wish to continue arguing with Anastasia. "Well, there is something I have to do." She started to explain why she wanted to leave early, but her sister wouldn't give her a chance.

"It's okay. I don't have to know what you do away from the winery. Your life is your life." Anastasia waved her sister aside, not wanting an explanation, just indicating her desire to work alone.

"I guess no one can ever get close to you."

"No one would want to." Anastasia laughed at herself. "I'm a work-driven, hard-headed, man-hating woman, or so you all say. How could anyone tolerate me?"

"Find the right man and you won't say that."

"I tried that already, as you know. Five years of marriage! Who needs another disaster? I have this problem that puts off most men."

"What problem? You're attractive and intelligent."

"Only a sister wouldn't notice. My right brain is a man; my left is a woman."

"I don't believe that for a minute."

"Never mind, Federica. Go home. Go take care of your husband or whatever you want to do. He's a good man, even if he is the only solid one in this family."

"Actually there is something I have to do. I was going to ask you if I could be away for a couple of hours."

"You don't have to explain to me."

"But I want to, Anna. It's about my son. I have to see his counselor at school."

"Is Sandy in some kind of trouble again?"

"Yes, as usual. I wish you would talk with him. He listens to you and sometimes his father, but lately I can't seem to get through to him."

"He's just headstrong. He'll find his way."

"I know, Anna. He's the son you should have had. Do you want to adopt him? I'll let him go at a discount."

Anna smiled and just waved her off. Federica didn't expect an answer anyway, so she turned off the steam pressure and coiled up the hose. She changed her rubber boots for running shoes. Even though it was not yet noontime, she left the winery for the short drive to the St. Helena middle school.

* * *

Joseph Pugliesi, grandson of Amerigo Pugliesi, also father of Federica and Anastasia, was fortunate enough to have inherited the *Immelhoff Winery*, including eighty acres, forty in grape vines. Other acreage contained walnut trees, the house, winery, barn and four shacks which had been upgraded to cabins for use by the itinerant workers. Another twenty of the acres consisted of the Emma Mae portion of the property whose vines consistently produced the best of the estate wines. The upper steep slopes of the Mayacamas could not be used for grape vines; but the lower acres, sloping to the foothills, were excellent for growing white wine grapes.

Amerigo had bought the exceptional twenty-acre Emma Mae Vineyard from his neighbor and named that section in honor of the man's daughter who died much too early in her young life. Joseph appreciated but never fully understood how much all of this meant to his immigrant grandfather.

Although he had been sent to the University of California at Davis where he graduated with a major in enology, Joseph also minored in business administration. He was not so sure he wanted to become a winemaker.

Before committing himself to the winery, Joseph thought he should explore the possibilities in and around the Bay area. He stayed in his stepfather's apartment in San Francisco near the marina and wandered into and out of all kinds of establishments. With encouragement from his uncle Giovanni, he tried the garment industry. That lasted a few days. He sipped cocktails and talked about possibilities with a whole gamut of upcoming young corporate types during the afternoon happy hours they seemed to need for relaxation. He signed on for several overnighters in small fishing boats. He visited the stock market, the city government offices, advertising agencies, the newspapers. None of these professions even remotely appealed to him. They all seemed a way of passing time until something real came along.

One day he wandered into one of the wineries that still operated within the city. There the odors and the activities hit him with a realization he'd never before experienced.

Until then, important choices had been made for him: his schooling, his direction, every thing which really mattered had been decided for him. So far he'd gone along taking the easy route, occasionally arguing a little, sometimes exerting token resistance, but always accepting the decisions others had made.

In an instant, struck by an epiphany while standing next to a giant redwood cask of aging red wine, he was transported by the aroma to his true home. Though the direction was obvious all along, this time entirely on his own, he made the most important yet the easiest decision he had ever made. He knew then and there what direction his life's work would take.

He immediately ran out to his brand new red Mustang convertible, which had been given to him as a graduation present, and drove back to the *Immelhoff Winery* where he related his experience to Amerigo. His grandfather accepted Joseph's decision without hesitation. In fact the old man never could comprehend how anyone, if he had the choice, could ever want any other kind of life.

Joseph stayed with his decision. He pitched in and willingly performed all forms of necessary labor, from the fields to the crush to the fermenting to the bottling, eventually becoming a competent winemaker. As that happened, Amerigo gave him more and of the responsibility. He did a good job of running the winery and keeping the operation solvent and competitive even after he became the sole owner.

A brown-eyed beauty came into his life through his contacts with one of the independent Sonoma grape growers. The girl's father owned a vineyard of Sangiovese grapes that Joseph occasionally bought and turned into one of his favorite wines.

He also drove over to Sonoma often enough to check on the readiness of the grapes, but really to get to know the grape grower's beautiful daughter. They were a perfect match, both born into the winemaking life and strongly attracted to each other.

Joseph did not have to make too many trips before proposing. They married in a small private ceremony, soon had two children; but tragedy struck with the second child. Joseph's lovely wife didn't survive Anastasia's birth.

He never completely recovered from that devastating loss. In the aftermath, he resisted several corporate offers to buy him out and fought to keep his winery independent while raising his daughters. Though the *Immelhoff Winery* never developed a wine with the reputation of a Mount St. Helena Chardonnay or a Stags' Leap Cabernet Sauvignon or a Robert Mondavi Opus One, Joseph Pugliesi remained a reputable working craftsman.

* * *

Federica was just getting into her car to leave the grounds, when her father drove in. She saw him and thought as usual, he's still the handsomest man in the entire Valley. Now in his late fifties, his hair was more gray than black. Time hadn't done too much to alter his lean body and pleasant smile.

"Hi, sweetheart. Leaving early?"

"Yes. I have to take care of some business with your grandson. Besides, Anna wanted to work alone."

"She driving you out?"

"You know her well, don't you?"

"Not well enough," Joseph admitted.

Federica raised her eyebrows, showing she understood the turmoil her sister was causing.

He leaned his head into the car window and kissed his daughter on the cheek, then went on into his office that adjoined the lab.

* * *

Joseph ran the business end of the winery with occasional forays into the actual making of the wine, especially during the crush and fermenting. After that most of his work had to do with operations: business meetings, advertising decisions, licensing problems, distribution policies, financial concerns, hiring and firing employees both permanent and temporary.

Since Anastasia had excelled in her studies at Davis, and showed extraordinary skill in winemaking with fervent interest in the entire process, her father encouraged her by allowing her to deal with many of the steps and decisions necessary during the pressing, bottling and aging of the wine.

For her it was not to be a gradual takeover. From the moment he had spoken the words, she had tried to assume complete control as though there never was any question of things being otherwise. She was perfectly willing to excuse her father's thirty-five years of experience, and proceed at full speed hell-bent on success, certain she knew what to do, where to go, and how to get there.

* * *

Anastasia didn't look up from her work, though she knew her father had walked in. She was studying the formation of the single-celled yeast they had been using to ferment the crushed grapes into wine. Without looking up, she spoke loud enough for her father to hear.

"Dad, what kind of yeast is this?"

He walked to the door of the lab. "You know it comes from our German supplier."

"But I asked you what kind it is. Do you even know?"

"If you need a name, I'll give you a phone number. What's the difference anyhow?" He turned away and headed back toward his desk.

"Will you wait a minute? I'm not drilling you. There is something I need to know."

Joseph waited for her to go on.

"How can you be sure this yeast will produce the best possible wine?"

"That was decided a long time ago. There's no need to question it."

"Isn't there a natural yeast on grapes?"

"Yes, of course, there are several. Any one of them might start fermenting right after the crush. But as you know, that's not a reliable way to make wine. That's why we stop it with the sulfites."

"But sometimes it turns out good without tampering, isn't that so?"

"Yes, sometimes, but more often than not it comes out bad. The practice is too risky."

"Then maybe I'm on to something."

"Care to explain?"

"Not till I'm sure I can carry this off. I have some more experimenting to do."

"Honey, experiment all you want. But you won't know until the wine ages if the yeast you used will make a good wine. That might take years to find out."

"That's typical of you. Give a little and pull away a lot."

"Only being practical."

"Don't fear. In the meantime, we'll go on using your German yeast and keep wondering why we're not making the best wine in the Valley."

Joseph started to protest that it was not his yeast. Instead he said, "You might develop a better yeast, and then again you might not. I get the feeling you would try anything just for the sake of trying. Everything new isn't necessarily better, you know."

"I said we'll continue using your yeast. Doesn't that satisfy you?"

"Tradition means nothing to you, does it?"

"The trouble with you, dear Father, is tradition means everything."

With that Joseph turned away and went back to his office wondering why these confrontations always left him so unsettled.

Anna picked up the wine thief she had been using, looked at it with hostility as though it was offensive, and then hurled it to the floor. The glass portion shattered on the concrete sending fragments and shards in a ragged circle.

Joseph heard the glass breaking, looked through the office window at his daughter, but decided not to interfere at that moment.

Anna retrieved a few pieces of the glass, strangely feeling as she did so that she was picking up shattered pieces of her life. When she bent over for a second handful of glass, she saw reflections of her broken marriage. Four years had passed since the separation, but confusion and bitterness were as hard to get rid of as tar on your feet after a wonderful day at the beach; one that began with bright sun and hope and ended with sticky traces of memories that couldn't be scraped away and emotions that never completely dissolved.

She wanted so badly for the marriage to work, one that seemed to have been the best solution for her at first, but then she found that marriage limited her freedom and she realized had also diminished her sense of control. Because Marco, her husband, was not a forceful person, might have been part of the problem. Whenever he attempted to assert himself, Anna flew into such a rage it took hours for her to get her emotions back under control. In the meantime he would sit back until the storm subsided, then relinquish the attempt and eventually just let her have her way.

Anna dropped the handful of shards into a basket. The noise gave her a momentary sense of relief, so she gathered more fragments and sent them smashing down on the others.

Joseph observed her behavior but made no move to question or interfere. He wondered what was happening to his once loving, lovely daughter. God, she's beautiful, he thought. Even when she's angry, which is most of the time now. Those deep, dark eyes look out with such fury at the world. What can I do to make things right?

Anna swept up the rest of the glass and dumped it into the wastebasket. She grabbed her jacket and hurried out to her Jeep Cherokee. The rear tires sent out two rooster tails of dirt and gravel into the air as she drove off.

* * *

Joseph had to take a walk outside to settle down. Leaves on neat rows of vines were turning from green to rust. A few remaining clusters of purple grapes lightly covered with gray mold were hanging from cane branches on the vines. He walked into the vineyard above the stone winery where a skeleton crew consisting of the vineyardist and three men were cutting the last clusters of ripe Cabernet Sauvignon with their sharp serpettes and carefully loading them into lug boxes to be taken to the crusher. They were clean-picking the vineyard so none of the ripe fruit would be overlooked.

Joseph knew, when the harvest was crushed and fermented, the grapes would willingly turn their sweetness into red wine mystique. Starting the fermentation was one of the most crucial aspects of winemaking. The beginnings pointed the way to the results. Sometimes good things happened. But he'd tasted wines developed from rich harvests that never achieved their potential. Like children who needed the right balance of guidance and freedom to reach their promise, wine was not always rewarding. The aroma of every fermentation simmered enigmatically prompting both expectation and apprehension, just one of the many concerns for every winemaker.

"Should be a great vintage," Oscar Mendez, the vineyardist, a field-experienced third generation Mexican American working for the *Immelhoff Winery*, said. "We have 24.2 balling on these little beauties."

"That's excellent. Check with Anna to see what she wants to do after you crush them. She'll decide how we'll handle the fermenting."

"You really trust her, don't you?"

"Yes, Oscar. I trust her completely. Don't try second-guessing her. She knows what she's doing."

"I hope you're right, señor. These late-harvest Cabernets could make one of your best wines ever."

CHAPTER 2

Two hours later, Anastasia parked outside the Pacific Central Bank, which her family used in San Francisco. She approached the new assistant loan manager. Donald Stanton smiled an easy grin and stood up behind his desk while Anna walked toward him with controlled determination in every step.

She saw a good-looking, slightly-built man about thirty, immaculately dressed in a light tan suit, matching well-polished shoes, light brown hair blow-dried and cut just so. His dress shirt displayed his first name embroidered above the pocket. The tie was the latest silk creation. Anna held off telling him what she thought about his too perfect attire: the suits, the hair, the shirts. They all seemed an affectation he didn't need. Why can't he just be a solid person, straightforward, honest and open, as she thought herself to be? But then she wondered why she even cared about his appearance.

"You're looking spiffy today," he greeted her, as he motioned for her to have a seat in front of his desk.

"In my jeans and work shirt? Get off it."

"You look good enough for me to take you out for lunch. It's getting late. Have you eaten?"

"Not today. I don't have time."

"Dinner tonight?"

Impatiently, she let out a sigh. "Look, I didn't come for a romantic tryst. The last time we talked, you told me about a way I could get control of my winery. That's what I want to discuss."

"Yes, I remember the discussion. I had been studying the outstanding loans I assumed with this job, but you hung up on me before I could explain because you said you were too busy to listen. Naturally I assumed you weren't interested."

"Isn't it possible I actually was busy?"

Donald sat down and gestured for Anna to do the same. But he didn't try to explain himself.

"Are you going to let me in on it," Anna pressed, "or was that just a ploy to have someone sit with you for lunch?"

He sat at the computer and slowly punched at a few keys, and then began: "Your father has a rather large loan for the new stainless steel tanks, which I understand you encouraged him to buy. At the time he didn't factor in the additional cost of installation. He also had to have two of the old tanks removed. You might not have realized the total cost is significant."

"Has he started payments?"

"Not necessary as of now. My predecessor and he agreed to delay payments until after this year's harvest."

"So what is this plan you have?"

"You have to get him to overextend, convince him he needs to expand to stay competitive. Have him buy more equipment. Better yet, get him to purchase another winery to increase business."

"And then?"

"He'll have to declare bankruptcy. We'll foreclose, and you can assume the debt, which would give you control of the business."

"That will never happen. First of all, Dad won't buy anything else until he pays off this current loan. That's the way he operates, and the way he will continue."

"Then you might have to find some other way to remove him from his position."

"So I drove to San Francisco to hear this nonsense? You really don't understand anything. I don't hate my father. The action you suggest would destroy him. I want to gain control of the winery, not send the man to a hospital."

"Well, I have been researching your family history, but I confess there remain a few matters I don't as yet know about you."

"Why would you research my family? Do you do that with all your clients?"

"Only up to a certain point, but you're not like all my clients. Tell you what, since you are here and you don't want lunch, why not take advantage of my offer for an early dinner? Pass some time doing a little shopping or whatever this afternoon. I'll meet you later, and we'll get to know each other better."

Anastasia's dark eyes could sparkle with warmth or they could as easily deliver a threatening message. This time she stared at Donald in a cold, dispassionate way. "You're a nice-looking man, almost too pretty. Maybe that's why I'm not attracted to you. You see, I was a sucker once for a handsome face—never again."

Donald ignored her last remark but seemed to be pleased by the compliment it contained. At least outwardly there was no apparent change in his manner. Without skipping a beat, he said, "Oh, yes, I meant to tell you, your ex, Marco, was here yesterday. We had lunch. I might be going into a partnership with him."

"You'd be the type."

"What do you mean by that?"

She refused to explain herself and just said, "Nothing good will come of it."

"Anna, you've never really understood the man you married. He's honest and hardworking."

"Also reliable, steadfast, consistent, and dependable. You see, I don't need you to defend him."

"Maybe not, but Marco's wine distribution firm is on the threshold of doing very well."

"With my wine I might add."

"Among others. You do have a contract with him. Why shouldn't he promote Immelhoff wines?"

"My father signed the contract, not me."

"You should be grateful. He has just expanded the Southeastern market. Big potential there. Immelhoff wines from Atlanta to San Antonio. How does that sound?"

"That's hardly news. We've been selling in the South for a long time."

"Not in the volume and for the prices you will get now. Marco is also a brilliant public relations man."

"So now you are a front man for Marco. Next you'll be telling me to take back my married name."

"He's a Preziano; for now, you're back to using Pugliesi. What's in a name? I've learned that a name can hide as much as it reveals."

"Are you being purposely enigmatic? Listen, I'm busy. If you ever come up with any decent ideas about how I can gain control of my winery, let me know. Otherwise, no more calls, please."

Donald smiled inwardly, knowing this would not be the last he would see of Anastasia. He thought he would toy with her a little. "I would rather you see me in the brightness of day when the sun brings forth hope; otherwise, darkness brings out the madness in man."

"You sound like a fool."

"Maybe, but I'm a wise fool who knows more about you than you might like to hear."

Anna stood, turned quickly away from him, and walked out to her Cherokee. Before firing up the engine, she sat in the vehicle for a while. She really didn't have the patience to grapple with the opaque nonsense he was spouting. One thing Donald said did stay in her mind. She had tossed it off at the time, but perhaps she should take a little more time before leaving San Francisco while she pondered the idea. She headed for a small sandwich shop on a side street off Market Square, which offered a tasty fresh eggplant sandwich with a smattering of sauce and a sprinkle of parmesan. Other than that, shopping, as Donald also suggested, was really not an option for her. In fact, the way many women spent their time browsing the stores for things they didn't really need struck her as a waste of time. But she was hungry, perhaps for something that might be satisfied from eating, more than likely it would not.

Her mind was wrestling with the one comment from Donald's remarks: "Find some other way." Maybe there was something she could do. Her plan might upset her father, but if it worked out he would realize how serious she was and perhaps give her the control she so desperately sought.

After eating, Anna did not drive directly back to the winery. She decided to put her plan into action immediately so took a short detour into Napa City. On the outskirts of the city near the slowly meandering Napa River, she pulled into the parking spaces of a small one-story commercial building. There was no office inside. She saw numerous layered stacks of wood staves along one wall. On the opposite wall stood a row of firepots, one of them burning with what smelled like fresh wood chips. A stout-bodied working man wearing a leather apron was setting a partially finished barrel over the heat. The man saw Anna enter, pulled the barrel off the fire, and set it down waiting for her to approach him.

"Hello, I'm Anastasia Pugliesi with the *Immelhoff Winery*."

He extended his roughened worker's hand. "Ahh, I know who you are. I'm Stavos, the cooper."

"And, of course, I know who you are. That's why I am here. I need almost immediately new oak barrels for this year's harvest. Can you help me?"

"Well, miss, usually I work on order, but I do have a couple dozen casks you could buy." He pointed to two rows of barrels lined against the back wall of the shop.

"Are they American or French oak?"

"These are American oak from New England. The man who ordered them had to change his mind. He's selling off his winery."

"Okay. I'll take them. Could you also make some for me with the French oak?"

"I can, but you realize that will take some time."

"How much time?"

"You come right to the point, don't you, ma'am?"

She didn't answer that question so Stavos said, "I have enough seasoned wood. If I enlist my son and hire extra help, I could manage to deliver in a few weeks."

"That would be fine. My wine is fermenting. I could use the few barrels you have ready now and let the rest of the wine remain in stainless steel for a while."

"Don't you already have cooperage? Your father visited me not too long ago, said he might need new barrels soon, but he was strapped for money right now."

"I didn't realize he came to see you. Well, this order will be paid for from my personal savings so he doesn't have to know about it, at least not for a while."

Stavos smiled, thinking that he understood Anna's meaning. "I'll send the two dozen I have and start on the new ones."

Anna wrote him a check for three thousand dollars and said, "This is a starter payment. I'll drop by after you let me know what the total cost will be. By the way, don't send these finished barrels for another week. Something I have to take care of first."

"How many new ones will you need?"

"Hold on." She clicked on her calculator and spoke while she was figuring. "If I let some of the wine rest in the tanks after fermenting, and move some of it inside to the redwood, let me see, sixty-gallon barrels from an eight-thousand-gallon tank, the others not quite full. Let's see; we'll probably use the new barrels for the Emma Mae wines but not Dad's Zinfandel. I'll already have the two dozen American oak by then. Okay, I want one hundred forty barrels of new French oak."

"I'll bet your father is very proud of you. I imagine he'll be surprised but happy about this new cooperage."

"I'm not so sure about that."

He smiled and shook her hand in both of his powerful leathery paws.

* * *

Anna drove from the Stavos Cooperage northward along the Silverado Trail. Operating just east of her in Wooden Valley was the Altamura Winery, which produced some of the best Sangiovese in Napa. She thought perhaps someday she might try making some of that full-bodied, satisfying, Tuscany-styled wine. That is, if she could ever achieve decisive control of her *Immeloff Winery*. She drove on through the Stags' Leap District with its fine Cabernet plantings and on to the Rutherford region, admiring undulating row after row of vines, thinking this Valley might not be Tuscany, but it certainly is as beautiful.

When she reached the road branching off to the Rutherford Hill Winery, she couldn't help reminiscing about the home on that twisting road where she lived with Marco until they broke up. She could almost not remember the reasons they parted. All she could say to herself now was that something was not quite right, so once again she should try to put it all behind her.

Actually Anna was still half-owner of the house that was situated just a block above the Silverado Trail. They had agreed Marco could live in the place until they sold the property, though so far they hadn't put it on the market. Right now, with all her plans, she could certainly use the money. Selling the house would be a definitive move, yet she was still not ready to pursue that course. Something about that move still unsettled her. As usual, Marco was no help in deciding. He was happy to stay where he was for as long as he could.

At Zinfandel Lane, she turned left and continued on across to Highway 29, the Old Wine Road, now heavy with traffic, and then onward north again to the Pugliesi-owned family winery.

She parked near the house, got out of the car, turned away from the winery and paced quickly up to the terrace where Oscar and his assistants were pumping the last of the must from the destemmer/

crusher into the smaller fourth stainless steel tank. She noticed Federica was there on hand as usual to start the fermentation process.

Anna never knew whether Oscar's vineyard workers were his relatives, or friends. At harvest times he hired most of his extended family including his wife, his daughter when she could get away from school, and other workers. Not that it mattered who they were because they were all reliable. But the thought passed through her mind that she felt she could always trust Oscar to choose good help. More than that, he had been the vinyardist since she was a child. He had always been a reliable person, a man she could talk with. Strange, she thought, that she could be at ease with him and not her own father or ex-husband.

Above the winery where the crusher and fermentation tanks were located, Oscar and Federica were discussing the harvest. He turned to face Anna. "Hello, Miss Pugliesi. We finished running the last of the late harvest Cabernet through the crusher. We pumped the must into the older tank, the open fermenter, as you suggested."

"You've done well, Oscar. I want you to know I appreciate all the work you and your assistants have done."

He acknowledged her but did not prepare to leave.

Federica then asked Anna an important question, "I used our traditional yeast for the Emma Mae Vineyard grapes; now what about this fourth tank with this late harvest picking? Are you ready for me to inoculate? Do you want me to get the yeast?"

"No, leave it alone. I have plans for that one."

Freddie gave her sister a quizzical look but refrained from asking why not.

Anna answered the question that was not asked: "Except for the second tank, the one Joseph will turn into White Zinfandel that he considers his prize creation, I will handle the fermentation from here on out."

She then turned her attention back to Oscar. "You and your crew have worked long hard days, Oscar. There'll be a bonus for you this season. Now, why don't you take off for the rest of the day? Have some kind of a post-crush celebration."

"Yes, miss. That's kind of you. We will. I just want to say this has been a good harvest. Look at the color, and taste the sweetness." He brought the tips of his fingers to his mouth. "These Cabernet grapes are so beautiful they were wiggling on the vines like beautiful girls tempting us to kiss them. I was telling your father, this late crop should make an outstanding wine, could be even better than the Emma Mae grapes."

"Right. I'm looking forward to seeing the results."

* * *

Anna had carefully analyzed the yeast which had formed and determined that it would work fine with her harvest of Cabernet Sauvignon grapes. It compared favorably with a natural mold she once studied that had occurred in a French vineyard. They called it noble rot and made an exceptional wine. She decided to use her natural yeast to start the fermenting for this late harvest crop. The next day and for several days afterward, she punched the cap down in the traditional manner. A few days later a little bubbling had occurred but not much else was happening with her experiment.

* * *

Marco drove up the driveway in his new Chevy pickup and headed for the winery.

"Damn!" She saw him walking toward the building so she left and went up to the row of stainless steel tanks.

Joseph was aware of why Anna suddenly walked out. He wanted to talk with her but thought it better if he waited a while because he didn't want her to feel he was interfering. He asked Marco to wait inside while he went up to the fermenting tanks where Anna was setting the temperature controls. He asked her if she would come back down into his office.

"Why is Marco here?" she demanded to know.

"Just business. Something we want you to hear."

Reluctantly she followed her father to the office, stopping outside long enough to stare her anger right through the glass partition at Marco before she entered.

Marco tried not to react, but her hostility knifed through his resistance. Tall for an Italian, with an athletic physique, Marco possessed a head of exceptionally thick dark hair, and facial hair that needed shaving twice a day to prevent it from looking like the beginnings of a black beard. Another unusual thing about him; his eyes were a soft light blue. They showed a sensitive side that Anastasia never understood. She mistook kindness for weakness and never really knew the man she had married.

As she looked at him, she had to admit again to herself that he was quite a handsome man. She even liked the dark brown corduroy jacket and casual light chino trousers he wore. Those are surface things, she told herself, and then saw that her father was motioning for her to join them.

She moved slowly enough to show her reluctance, but finally did go on into the office. She glanced at Marco without a greeting and waited for her father to explain why she was called.

"Marco has been doing some meaningful work for us. He's expanding our market in the South."

"I know," she said. "Georgia to Texas and all points in between."

"How did you know that? Marco just now told me."

"I heard it from Donald Stanton who also told me that he and Marco might become business partners. Any truth to that?" she asked her ex.

"Yes, we're considering working together on a project," Marco admitted.

"I'd be wary of that pretty-faced slicker if I were you."

"You're wary of everyone."

"Marco, sweetheart, you are so naïve. You'd be a pushover for anyone as aggressive as Donald."

"Oh, are you on a first name basis now?"

"Whatever. It's none of your business. You don't own me anymore."

"I never owned you at any time in our lives, nor did I even try," Marco defended himself as calmly as he could.

"No, an indecisive person like you never could."

"Never indecisive," he said, "only patient with all your whims."

"You see, you can't tell a resolution from a whim."

"Well, you throw your resolutions around faster than sixth graders in a rotten-apple fight."

"As I remember that was how you first caught my attention."

"Even then you were always so serious. Besides"—Marco had to laugh at his own thought—"I was an older eighth grader. You should have ducked."

"You're incorrigible!"

"No. I'm encourageable."

Joseph had to break in. "Wait, you two. We're not in a war here. We all have the same goals."

"No," Anastasia corrected her father, "your goal is to survive. My goal is to move away from your popular wines to the finest wine ever crafted in this Valley."

"Well, popular wines bring in the revenue," Joseph reminded her. "The luxury wines you are talking about will never sell in volume."

"Your father is right, Anna. But actually, you could do both," Marco suggested.

"Now you're going to tell me how to run our operation?"

"No. I'm just trying to tell you that the two methods are compatible. The Greeks believed one could achieve harmony by moderation in all things, a sound mind in a sound body."

"And that *sounds* like you, always ready to compromise."

"Compromise just goes with the human condition."

"Maybe so, but we're not."

"We're not what?" he asked.

"Compatible!" she threw the word at him.

Marco sucked in his feelings, and said, "It doesn't have to be that way."

"If what?" she asked.

"If you would just step back and take a close look at yourself."

"I see. I'm to blame now?"

"No. You've never been to blame for anything in your life . . . sweetheart!"

Joseph tried to intervene again: "Let's not get into that area of blaming each other."

"No, let's just continue the chaos."

"No, Anna. That's not what I want at all," Marco said. "Since we're all in this business together, we should be able to work things out."

"No, it's really you two against one. Well, I'll tell you this one is not backing off. I have plans for this winery, and none of you will block my way."

Marco shook his head and looked to Joseph for support when he said, "Being a CEO isn't enough for her. This woman won't stop until she's a full-fledged goddess."

"Right. I like that," Anastasia said. "Goddess of the Valley."

"There already was a Greek goddess: Demeter Goddess of Agriculture. You are probably just a misplaced Greek anyhow. Why not call yourself Wine Goddess of the Valley?"

"Hey, Wine Goddess of the Valley. I could live with that."

"But not with me?" Marco asked without expecting an answer.

CHAPTER 3

No deer, no cougars, no wild horses, no Pomo or Patwin Natives are running free in the Mayacamas or anywhere across the Valley's floor. The Valley, now known as Napa, was Indian for home. The early discovery of quicksilver and silver in the 19th century brought in scores of miners who quickly excavated the ore and crowded out the early inhabitants. Later cattle and walnuts, wheat and peaches grew on the fertile sloping earth until they succumbed to acres of varietal grapes planted in row after row on the rich volcanic soil between the mountains even up onto the rising slopes. Throughout the 20th century, the weather, the land, and the immigrant flow all coalesced to emerge into a wine-producing terrain like no other on earth.

The Napa Valley, three miles wide and thirty-some miles long, was not simply carved out by water flowing between the mountains. The moving tectonic plates have been pulling the mountains apart with the events of the San Andreas network of faults. Evidence of this cataclysmic work are most obvious at the northern end of the Valley where heated groundwater shoots geysers up through fissures and settles down into mud baths with supposedly medicinal properties.

One can begin to understand why Anastasia, raised in this tumultuous environment and earning a living from the product of the same soil, might be constantly on the verge of eruption. How could she not be explosive when the elemental forces under and all about her were in a constant state of unpredictable movement?

* * *

Anastasia awoke in the morning feeling none the worse for yesterday's arguments with Marco and her father. Since the breakup of her marriage, she had returned to live in the family's home. She shared the kitchen with her father, but used the large bedroom, bath, and separate rear entrance, which years before had been added on to the original house.

During the night, Anna had received a visitor. When she heard the key turning the lock on the door, she switched off the television set and sat in the dark waiting. She was expecting the man. He entered the room quietly and walked directly to her but said nothing. Placing his hands under her arms, he lifted Anna from the chair. She stood up to him. The first kiss was a greeting, the second a longer statement of desire. There seemed little reason to speak for they both knew what each wanted. They embraced passionately, and then he helped her out of her robe and pajamas. When she was totally undressed, she unbuttoned his shirt and undid his trousers. He stepped out of his shorts and led her gently to the bed.

They faced each other. She placed her fingers over his mouth so he wouldn't say the things he wanted to say. She kissed his lips and pressed against his body, then willingly submitted. They made love that came slowly at first and rose with a quiet crescendo to an intimate, passionate intensity. He held off, waited, waited, until she was ready.

After, exhausted and fulfilled, Anna lay back and relaxed. "I don't know what I'm going to do about you."

"You can keep me here permanently if you like," the man suggested.

"No. In the morning, I'd have to explain everything to my father."

"At your age you don't have to explain anything to anyone."

"I suppose you are right," she said but did not indicate she would change her mind.

"You could live somewhere else, rent a condo, or better yet come to live with me. I have plenty of room."

"No, I won't do either. I love this home. It is my link to my great grandfather, the only connection I have to a culture I've never really known, but desperately need. You see, my father thinks I don't respect tradition, but there is nothing I would treasure more than to be able to live in the ways of the old country."

"Anna, Anastasia, you have more needs than I can ever understand. I'll try to be here for you, if you let me."

"I know you will. It would be better now if you just leave."

Resigned, he said, "Of course, if you're sure that's what you want."

She did not respond. While he was dressing, Anna began to feel that she was descending into a darkness from which she could not escape. "You will you come back, won't you?" she asked, more desperately than she had intended.

"If you let me, I'll return, or I'll stay on right now."

"No, don't press me. I can't allow you to stay." She placed both palms against her forehead and rubbed slowly. "I think you'd better go."

"You're getting sad, aren't you?"

She did not answer, and they did not say goodbye. He embraced and kissed her in a way that said he did not want this be the last of their meetings. Then he went quietly out the door, walked down the driveway and along the road to where he had parked his car.

Anna couldn't give in to the emotions that were consuming her while her lover was there. As soon as he was gone, Anna covered her face with a pillow, hoping her father wouldn't hear the sobs and sighs, which arose from somewhere deep within her being. Her emotions burst the dam she had built to contain them, and the flood went down her face and neck until she went into the bathroom and tried to wash it all away with cold, clear water.

She returned to her empty bed. Eventually she drifted into a sleep with no dreams, but gained the restoration that came from letting go of her cares for a few hours.

* * *

In the morning, after getting herself ready for the day, Anna strolled into the kitchen where she prepared toast and a poached egg for herself. Her father had started the coffee earlier and came back into the kitchen.

"Hi, Dad. Like a poached egg this morning?"

Joseph didn't really want any eggs, but Anna was being so cordial about it, he couldn't refuse. He poured coffee for both of them and sat down to wait for the egg.

"Toast, too?"

"Sure, honey. What's on your schedule today?"

"First thing is not to argue with you or your friend Marco. You know I wish you would let him go, but I understand you like the results he gets. I even have to admit, he's a good salesman, probably because he is kind of handsome so he makes a good impression, like an attractive window display."

Now Joseph knew they were on slippery footing. Not that Anna couldn't be sweet. He just hadn't seen it in her behavior for a long while. If he defended Marco at this time and told her how he thought she should get back together with him and that she would never find a better man, he would quickly lose ground in this tug of war.

"You know, Dad, I've been thinking about our discussion regarding the yeast we use. I'm not giving up on finding the best strain possible you understand, but you are probably right. It might take years. We'll see. However, there is something we could do right away that would make a difference."

Joseph sipped his coffee and waited, remembering a time he walked across a pond with rubber ice. The surface moved up and down with every step. At any moment he knew he could break through and be plunged into the icy water.

"Cork can do more to hurt a wine than bad cooperage," she said.

"We use good cork. What are you suggesting?"

"Wine is held in by cork for months while it's in the wood and then again for years when in the bottle. If it's improper, allows too much oxidation, too many oils or the wrong bacteria growing in the fibers, it can introduce cork flavor or even spoil the bottle or a whole barrel."

"I know, Anna. But that rarely happens. We always use the best cork from Portugal and Spain."

"Actually the best come from Sardinia, but that's not why I raised the subject." She served him the poached egg and toast, and let him start eating before she continued. "In an experiment conducted in Europe with a good wine barrel-aged and then bottled for the same length of time with different containment techniques, the corked wine finished last. A synthetic material finished first."

"I would question whether that experiment was handled properly. Wine needs oxidation. Plastic can't give it that."

"Not plastic, synthetic. Wine doesn't react to the material and proper oxidation takes place through a honeycomb of passages."

"I don't know about trying synthetics. I hate to tamper with a proven winner."

"How can we ever improve our wines if you refuse to change your methods?"

"Ah, now I'm wrong because I buy the best cork available. Sometimes, Anna, you are impossible."

"No. I deal with the possible. You are impossible. Wait!" She checked herself. "I vowed not to argue. Forget I ever said anything about cork or yeast or barrels."

"Barrels?"

"Never mind. I was thinking about a conversation I had yesterday with Federica."

"Is there something wrong with our barrels? If so, you should let me know. We are just about to put some of the harvest from the new fermenting tanks into them."

"No, nothing wrong, except they're tired and should have been put out to pasture a long time ago. But don't worry about that. We'll have the same results we had last year."

"Which was not our best financially, but not a bad year by any standards."

"Yes, not bad, if you're willing to accept mediocrity."

"Our wines are certainly not mediocre."

"No, they're fine, just fine. I'm going out to check the fermentation on the fourth tank, the late harvest Cab. I think we're not more than a day or two away from going to the press. After, please don't mess with the microfilter. I'll be careful to leave the sediment in the tanks. When the time comes, I'll rack off the lees. I don't even want to use the centrifuge. You damage the wines with all that spinning and filtering. I might even use your Grandpa Amerigo's technique for filtration: egg whites or bull's blood. Would that be tradition enough for you?"

"You're the winemaker, Anastasia. You make the final decisions."

"Yes, well, we'll see."

* * *

Federica's tall, vigorous, athletic, handsome, usually agreeable husband, Scott Anderson, came into the kitchen of their low ranch-style home. Federica wasted no time informing him that she had to visit their son's school and sit in on a discipline session for him and two of his friends.

"What did they do?" he asked.

"They were caught in the boiler room smoking cigarettes."

"Marijuana?"

"No. Regular cigarettes. But don't make light of it because they were also cutting class."

"What did the school officials do?"

"The assistant principal gave them all detention. But that's only a slap on the wrist. I want you to talk to Sandy. He's getting off on the wrong track. He leaves here every morning on time, but manages to be late almost every day."

"Where is he right now?" Scott asked.

"He had to stay late. That's the detention."

"He hates school, so they make him stay longer. I hardly think that will help."

"That's why you have to talk with him. I don't want him sent to a reform school or some such place."

"I doubt that it will come to that."

Federica set the table and served up their dinner. Sandy came shuffling in, dropped his backpack on his bed and came quietly into the dining room. He'd already heard from his mother earlier, so he kept looking toward his father wondering if he was in for it.

Scott acknowledged Sandy when he first sat at the table. He ate quietly, said nothing to his son until they finished the meal followed by a good frozen yogurt dessert, and then he turned to his wife. "That was an excellent dinner, honey." Finally, he spoke to Sandy. "Did you thank your mother?"

"No, but her dinners are always good, anyhow."

"Don't you think you should let her know?"

"I guess."

Scott chuckled at his son's lack of understanding. "Let's take a walk, Sandy."

"I have to do my homework."

"You'll have time. C'mon, walk with me."

Once outside, Scott was first distracted from his primary purpose of talking with his son. Bulldozers were knocking off the top of a nearby hill in preparation of putting up another two- or three-storied, would-be mansion. Scott shook his head in disgust but soon got his thoughts back to having that talk with his son.

He began a little awkwardly, "How old are you now, Sandy?"

"You know," the boy said. "I'm eleven."

"Right, of course. Mom said you got in trouble at school, caught smoking."

"Yeah. It was nothing."

"Did you like it?"

"Like what? You mean getting caught?"

"No. I mean did you enjoy smoking?"

"Not really. It goes up in your nose and smells bad, made my eyes water, too."

They walked around a corner and saw still another monster house going up. Scott continued talking with Sandy. "Why did you do it then?"

"You know. I wanted to see what it was like."

"Is this your first time?"

"Not really."

"That's an honest answer. I like that. Why did you try it this time?"

"Well, you know, I mean, one of my friends had some loose cigarettes and wanted us to have a smoke."

"So you went along, not because you wanted to but because your buddies were going to smoke?"

"I guess so."

"What if your buddies said they wanted to jump off a tall building? Would you do that?"

"Heck no."

"Why not?"

"Well, I don't want to get hurt or nothing."

"I see, but you don't think smoking will hurt you?"

"Not like jumping off a building."

"Not right away, anyhow."

Sandy looked up at his father and said, "Okay, I see what you're getting at."

"That's good, son. I don't want to lecture you; just keep one point in mind. This is only the beginning. You have to make tough decisions all your life."

"And you think I should worry about what happens afterward."

"Right on!" Scott gave his son a high five before they turned another corner and headed back home.

* * *

The next morning Scott came into the kitchen right after shaving. "Where's Sandy?"

"He left early for school," Federica said, "even seemed eager to go. You must have had a good talk."

"We did, but we'll have to see if it takes hold."

"How long before we'll find out?"

"Oh, maybe when he's thirty or so."

Federica was not willing to see any humor in that remark. "I certainly hope not."

Instead of sitting at the table to drink his first cup of coffee, Scott stood gazing out of the window. "Freddie, next time we buy a house, we'll get one next to a state park or a national forest."

"Why do you say that, honey?"

"Look what they're doing on the hill over there. They're bulldozing the walnut trees."

"I know, but aren't they going to put in grapevines?"

"These *lifestylers* come in from San Francisco and Southern Cal, overpay for a sector of land, knock off the hilltop for a gaudy, cheaply built mansion with a view, then cut up the land around it for a few rows of wine grapes."

"Are you in a bad mood this morning?" Federica asked.

"Not after last night." Scott raised his eyebrows over a mischievous smile.

"I didn't think so."

He kissed her on the neck, and then moved away from the window to sit at the table.

Federica filled his cup with wonderfully aromatic coffee and set a plate of sausage and scrambled eggs in front of him.

While he was buttering his toast, Scott said, "Let me tell you a story that Marco told me about one of the Valley's residences. He said it was believed that a deer, a huge eight- or ten-point stag, leaped into and out of the vineyards. Apparently not too many people ever saw it, but a legend was formed around it."

He paused to eat a few bites while Federica waited for him to continue.

"Each time the stag devoured some of the grapes, the vines in the entire field responded by yielding the sweetest grapes of the season.

The old-time growers began looking forward to the visits, hoping the deer would choose their property."

"Wouldn't all the other fields be affected?"

"No, just the ones the stag had visited. You know," he went on, "I wouldn't mind having Marco over for dinner some evening. We could have a glass of wine and one of those good conversations. It's been a while."

"That would be fine by me. Sandy seems to enjoy talking with him, too." She noticed that Scott moved into some serious eating, so she assumed the story was finished. "What's your job today?" she asked.

"One of the refrigeration tanks at the Sterling Winery is misbehaving. I'll have to check it out first and then probably return to my shop to get whatever items it'll need for repair. Of course, I could put it off for a couple of hours, if you have something else in mind."

"You oversexed mastodon."

"You didn't seem to mind last night."

"Just doing my wifely duties."

"Is that so! Who started it all?"

"Never mind." She nibbled a piece of dry toast and washed it down with orange juice.

"What's on your agenda?" he asked.

"Besides working for my sister, I'm always trying to get her back together with our father. You know, Scott, I don't trust her right now."

"What d'you mean?"

"She might do something drastic."

"Such as?"

"I don't know. Could you come over to talk with her?"

"Me?"

"Yes. She respects you."

"Maybe so, but if I just walked in, she'd be on her guard."

"We might work out something. Our bottling machine needs attention. It's getting cranky. It stops and starts, and then gets out of alignment so the corks won't set right. We could hire you to rebuild it before our next bottling."

"Okay, I can probably make the bottler cooperate, but I can't promise the same for your sister."

"You've known her and Marco for a long time."

"Anna and Marco? I thought the problem was with your father."

"It is, of course, but the real problem is with Anna and men, all of them."

"Except me?"

"Except you because you're out of circulation."

"And if I weren't?"

"Then she would detest you, too—like she does all the others."

"Poor Anastasia."

"See, at least you're sympathetic. Please come by and talk with her."

"Okay. I don't know how long it might take me today at Sterling, but after, I'll have another look at your relic of a bottler. How many times have I fixed it already?"

"Only seven or eight."

"A miracle it stills runs at all. Why don't you get your dad to buy a new one?"

"Not this year. He bought the new refrigeration tanks and had them set up. Of course no one consults me about these matters anyhow, but I think we're in debt."

"How could that . . . ?" Scott stopped the question because he disliked hearing problems about money and financing. If he had his way, he'd do the work he enjoyed doing and not charge for any of it, so long as he had food and a good roof for Federica, his son and himself. Everything else was fluff. "Didn't you want to hear the rest of the story?"

"About the deer? I thought you were finished."

"No, there's more." But instead of telling her, he devoured his breakfast, kissed her affectionately and went out to work.

* * *

The staff at Sterling Winery greeted Scott as they would a family member. He quickly located the problem with their refrigeration tank, so he drove immediately into St. Helena, got the new compressor, returned and installed it quicker than expected. On his home route he thought he'd stop off at Immelhoff's as he had promised to have a look at their ancient bottler. Federica was outside on the upper terrace checking the fermentation on the Chardonnay.

"Hi, Freddie. Nice to see you working."

She waved to her husband but didn't come down from the upper level. "Have a nice talk with Anna, if you can."

"Right," he agreed and went into the venerable stone building.

Anna was in her lab studying a professor's paper on botrytis cinera. As she read, she ran her fingers absentmindedly through her thick auburn hair. When she saw Scott walk in, she set the pamphlet down. "What do you know about the noble rot?"

"Enough not to get it between my toes."

"Always the joker," she said.

"Just want to enjoy everything while I can."

"There's a professor at Davis who has researched the California method of using natural mold to start the wine."

"That's okay if you want to make sweet wines."

"So you do know something about developing wine, don't you?"

"I've lived in this valley all my life. I have seen enough success and failure not to try to become a vintner. Besides, I don't have the patience for it. When I repair a centrifuge, I can see the results right then instead of waiting two or three years to find out if I did the right thing."

"Fair enough. What brings you here today?"

"Freddie tells me you're having trouble with the bottler."

"Why would she say that? We haven't tried using it yet this season. We won't need the bottler for a while until we give a little more time to what we have in the old barrels and the redwood."

"Guess she was looking ahead. You know, anticipating problems."

"More likely she wanted you to come here to have a talk with me."

"About what?"

"My erratic ways. I know she thinks I'm getting a bit loose in the skull."

Scott smiled knowing that Anna would not misinterpret his good intentions. "Have you had a man in your life lately?"

"That is none of your business."

"Just a friendly question. Mind if I have a look at the bottling machine?"

"No. It probably does need attention."

"Your bottler is as temperamental as its operator. I'll check it out."

"And then check me out!" Anna threw her head back with a defiant gesture. "Maybe you can order some new parts, so you can smooth out some of my rough edges, too."

"Anna, I've always liked your spirit. I understand mechanical things, but high-strung women like you who can run a winery or a corporation. No way. I just want to stay back and admire."

"Didn't you ever dream to be the best in your profession?"

"You mean, like run a huge company, crawl up a mountain of paper money?"

"Well, not just going after money, but rising to the top of what you do?"

"Not for me, I'm a blue collar worker. What I'm doing is fine: your beautiful sister, my restless son, good honest work. I'm living the dream."

"That's a smooth answer, Scott, but didn't you come here to give me advice?"

"Well, your sister is concerned; however, seeing you here operating in your own environment, I'm not worried. I don't think you're on a collision course, so I'll hold off giving advice unless I think it's necessary."

"Finally found a man who knows how to tame a woman."

"Oh, you're not wild enough to need taming."

"Thanks. I think that's a compliment."

"I better have a look at the bottler." He walked over and started examining its operating peculiarities.

She shook her head and went back to her reading. Just then, a slim, very attractive, dark-haired teenaged girl came cautiously into the winery. Anna motioned for her to come near.

"My father said he thought you'd be here working. May I speak with you?"

"Of course. I know who you are. You're Leticia, Oscar Mendez's daughter. You've grown into a very pretty young lady."

"Thank you. I hope you won't laugh at me, but I want to learn winemaking. Will you teach me?"

"Yes, I could, but in this business you have to learn from the ground up and also have some formal education."

"I've worked with my father in the vineyards, trimmed the canes, harvested the grapes. Wouldn't that count?"

"It certainly would. Actually I've seen you in the fields with your father and cousins."

"My father knows how to grow grapes, and tend to the vines. I love the land just like he does, but I want more than just working on it. I want to be like you. I want to make wine that people will love. Not for them to get drunk, but to appreciate life more. Do you know what I mean?"

"Yes, Leticia, I do. Have you thought about college after you finish high school?"

"Yes, I heard U.C. Davis is one the best places to learn the technical side of winemaking."

"You are right about that. When the time comes, I would be willing to write a letter of recommendation to help you get accepted."

"Thank you. I'm so glad I talked with you."

"I think you might have the makings a fine vintner. I could let you start by working with my sister Freddie if you like, and you will be paid."

"I'd like that. I could come in afternoons, maybe weekends, and a lot more during summer vacations."

"You can plan that out with Freddie. She's outside working up on the terrace today."

"Good. I've talked with her a lot of times. She's very nice."

"But you've never tried to talk with me before."

"I don't know how. You're kind of on another level. I didn't know if you would talk with me or not."

"Wow! That surprises me. I never thought I had that effect on people."

"I hope I didn't insult you."

"Not at all. You just opened my eyes to something I should know. I'd like to have you working with us here, Leticia. I just might be able to learn from you."

After Scott had finished examining the bottling machine, he came over to speak with Anna.

"Scott, this is Leticia Mendez, Oscar's daughter. We're going to take her on as an apprentice. She'll start by working with Freddie; that is, when she can find time away from school."

Leticia showed her agreement with a beautiful smile and shook Scott's hand. "Your wife is a very nice lady."

"I think so, too."

She left the winery and went up to tell Federica her good news.

"Well, what did you find out about our bottler?" Anna asked Scott.

"The machine will continue to serve you like the wonderful one-hoss shay. Though I doubt it'll last a hundred years and a day, but it will probably disintegrate all at once. In the meantime, I tightened the tension on the belt. It doesn't need replacing any more than the rest of the machine. I also aligned the nozzle with the bottling track so the corks can be sufficiently compressed before being inserted. I'll explain to Freddie how to reset it all if it falls off kilter again."

"Thank you. I learned something about myself by talking with Leticia. Now, from our conversation, what did you learn about me?"

"From my calculation, you're better off than Freddie thought, but not as bad as you seem to think."

"So what's the solution to my problem?"

"Like the bottler, you might come apart all at once."

"Care to elaborate?"

"Look, Anna, you really have a wonderful chance for a great career here. Don't blow it by doing something foolish."

"Such as?"

"I don't know. What did you have in mind?"

"Still have in mind," she said.

"That's all the explanation you're going to give?" Scott asked.

"When I have a mechanical problem, I'll call on you, Scott." She kissed him on the cheek to prove she wasn't angry with his none-too-subtle probing. "I'll handle things here. You keep the home fires burning."

"When your sister is at home, that's always a pleasure."

"Get out of here, you male chauvinist."

"Just on the surface." Scott left smiling his friendly smile. Outside, he waved at his wife but didn't go up onto the terrace where she was talking with Leticia.

Federica couldn't help wondering if he'd made any progress. She called down to him, "Accomplish anything?"

"I'll talk to you tonight."

CHAPTER 4

A flawlessly clean black BMW came up the driveway and pulled to a stop outside the winery. Donald Stanton wearing designer jeans, a tailored leather jacket, and highly polished black loafers, slowly got out of the car. Before he could go into the winery, another vehicle, Joseph's wine-colored Lincoln sedan, slid to a stop beside the Beamer.

"Mr. Pugliesi, I wasn't really expecting you."

"Didn't expect me at my own winery?"

"That's not really what I meant. I thought, well, I thought maybe I'd check on our investment. You do know I've been given full responsibility for your account. Would you mind if I call you Joseph? Pugliesi doesn't sound quite right for you. I am a Stanton, you know? Does that name sound familiar to you?"

"Only since I've met you."

"Of course. I expected that. Well, how are the new tanks working out?"

"You'll have to ask Anna. She's the winemaker."

"Yes, I'll do that."

Joseph hadn't thought about it before, but this Donald Stanton seemed to have some peculiar ways about him. Maybe he's just nervous about the account. But he seems more cocky than nervous, he reasoned as he went on into his office.

Instead of going into the winery, Donald walked around and up to the level of the fermentation tanks. He looked at them, and as much as he knew, they looked all right. What he really wanted to know, he wouldn't find out by simply looking at the large, bright stainless steel structures. Though he never revealed these thoughts to anyone else, during some private moments of reflection, he was pursuing more than a romantic interest in Anna or the winemaking process.

Anna's previous rebuke caused him to keep a certain distance, so one of the reasons for this visit was to find a way for her to open herself to him.

Actually he respected Marco more than he did Anastasia. Something in her nature he couldn't understand. He wondered why she and Marco didn't get back together again. They seemed right for each other. He was not convinced it would never happen. But whether they were finished as a couple or not really wouldn't alter his intentions. He saw no harm in trying once again to get on a good footing with the volatile young woman.

She was sitting, lost in thought, when he walked into her lab. At first she was not even aware of him as she was so focused on her concerns.

He said nothing to disturb her, and he didn't feel a bit awkward violating her privacy that way.

Eventually, she acknowledged his presence.

"I don't quite know how to proceed," Donald said.

"What are you doing here?"

"I better be straight with you. I told your father I came to check on the bank's loan."

"Did you?"

"Yes, I did. I mean I did check on what you've done with the investment, but that's not my primary reason for being here."

"What is?"

"Well, I came to find out if I might be able to have a talk with you."

"Whatever for?"

"The last time we spoke at the bank, I might have been too abrupt, too pushy."

"No, you made yourself clear. You wanted to take me out for dinner and whatever else might occur. I thought I made myself clear that I wasn't interested."

"You did, of course. But, for one thing, I would like to learn more about this winegrowing business, and I would like to get to know you better."

"As far as winemaking, you can read about that. As for getting to know me, nothing has changed."

"I believe we might have a chance to work things out. We could be much closer than you think."

"I'm flattered, but the answer is still no."

"Even if I were able to restructure the financing so you could get what you want?"

"You should listen to yourself, Donald, and you'd understand why I could never be interested in you. You want to foreclose on my father so I'll somehow become enamored of you. How romantic!"

"I was just testing you with that. I'm really trying to tell you that I'd do anything, almost anything, to win your respect. Why don't we have lunch today?"

"Listen to yourself again. Your commitment is as solid as a rain-soaked hillside. Anyone foolish enough to build on it would certainly find themselves sliding down to oblivion."

"Why do you have this callous attitude toward me?"

"Take that shiny leather jacket you're wearing. You probably think it makes you look rustic. Actually it makes you look like someone from Hollywood out of place in the wine country. Isn't that patent leather?"

"Certainly not! It's genuine, just like me."

"So you say. Well, tell you what, Donald, since you drove this far, yes, why don't you take me out to lunch? We can cement our relationship over a corned beef sandwich."

"Suddenly you want to go out for lunch? I guess I really don't understand you."

"You will. By the time we spread mustard on the bread, you won't want to see me again."

"It doesn't have to be like that."

"Oh, but it is like that."

"Then, of course, the invitation is off."

"That's the first good thing I've ever heard you say."

"Do you realize we're fighting like a couple of siblings? Don't you think it's possible that I might have other than a romantic interest in you?"

"No, I don't. Goodbye. I have work to do."

Donald threw up his hands to pretended frustration and walked away.

* * *

When Federica came in to work the next morning, she wanted to talk about her son. So without noticing what Anna was doing, she started right in: "I don't know what I'm going to do with Sandy." Anna listened but didn't respond. Federica went right on anyhow. "He's been behaving so well lately that I know he's up to something. This morning he suddenly says he wants a digital camera, an SLR no less."

"Is that so wrong?" Anna asked.

"He already has a bicycle that keeps him away from home hours at a time. Where would a camera take him, to the Pacific Ocean and back?"

"What does Scott say?"

"You know Scott. He's so easygoing he won't try to stop the kid."

What Federica hadn't noticed was that Anastasia had a hammer in one hand and was waiting for her to finish her complaint so she could use it. "How do you get these metal hoops off the damn barrels?"

Federica's shocked expression was enough for Anna to offer an explanation: "I'm planning to take the damned barrel apart."

"Why would you do that?"

"I want to show you the insides." Anna then slammed the hammer against the metal, knocking out a chunk of wood without moving the retaining hoop.

"You are ruining that barrel. Let me show you." Federica pried under the hoop with a dull chisel and tapped it upward with a hammer, moved the tool around, tapped again, and continued until the metal slipped off. With that done, the stays loosened up enough for her to remove the flat wooden top. They could then see inside the barrel. The wood was purple-stained with layers of residue.

"You see what I mean?" Anna said. "The lees are so ingrained in the wood no one can tell how many times this barrel was used or how effective it would be in giving oak flavor to the wine."

"I can check my records."

"Never mind records. You can tell from looking they are way past their prime. They should be retired." Anna knocked the lower metal hoop off and gathered up the loose staves which she threw into a pile.

"Wait! It isn't necessary to take the entire barrel apart to shave the insides. We'll have a hard time fitting those staves back together."

"Freddie, will you forget about these barrels? You're not going to do anything with them. In fact, I'd like you to roll the empty barrels out here. We need to make room for the Emma Mae Vineyard Cabernet Sauvignon that we will be barrel-aging soon. Right now I'm deciding something important here. If you don't mind, let me struggle with my thoughts."

Federica hesitated, then asked, "Before I get to the cellar work, do you want me to pump the fermenting wine over the cap in that fourth tank? I'm not sure what's going on with that one. I wish you'd take a closer look at it."

"I will as soon as I can." Anastasia's mind was already on something else, but she brought it back to answer the question. She spoke softly as though Federica was the one struggling with a difficult problem. "Yes, pump the wine over the cap but keep the pressure light. I've been punching it down, but that isn't working. I was hoping we could just punch it down like the old-timers did and not have to do all that pumping over the cap."

"But that would take us back to the days when they stomped the grapes with their feet."

"I like it when you get brave enough to talk back, Freddie. You see, what I really want is to blend the techniques that made some exceptional wines in the past with our modern-use technology. Now, please take care of the cap and then come inside to clear some room in the cellar while I chart our future."

Federica wanted to stay because she sensed her sister was under some kind of unusual stress. "Are you all right? I've never seen you quite like this before."

She heard Anna mumble, "Never mind, I'll be fine."

Reluctantly, Federica went outside through the large tall doors, then up to the stainless steel fermentation vats, shaking her head about the uncertainty she felt coming from Anna.

* * *

A university-educated, young Chinese American man had been foreman and translator for the workers who dug the tunnels into the hillside, literally at the foot of the Mayacamas. He also designed a ventilation and drainage system to allow use of the tunnels as both cellar and storage areas.

The same Chinese workers who had dug the cellars years before had also leveled and paved a slice of the surface outside and slightly higher than the winery. That section held the new fermenting tanks and the still-usable old one.

Anna and Federica's great grandfather, Amerigo, was the one who had conceived the plan so that gravity could be used to pull the fermented fluid through large pipelines down through the building directly to the redwood vats or the oak barrels, whichever they chose to use for aging the wine.

Later an immigrant stone mason with the help of his sons had laid the foundation layer by layer, building the stone walls for the winery outward from the same hillside which contained the three tunnels. The mason reserved the setting of the critical keystone to his own well-trained skills. The all-important centerpiece gave stability to the entire structure since it held pressure from both sides arching up to the head of the large entrance to the main building. His two boys then had the job of constructing two tall swinging doors that would allow vehicles or vats of great capacity into or out of the structure. The workmanship of both the tunnels and the winery had weathered a bit but held up fine for several decades.

* * *

While Federica worked outside, she could dimly hear thumping sounds reaching her through the venerable stone walls.

Anastasia hadn't waited for her sister to move the old barrels out of the tunnel. She rolled them out herself and then found a more efficient way of opening the barrels. Using a ten-pound sledgehammer, she smashed in the flat, round barrel tops. That immediately loosened the retaining hoops so she could knock them off and throw the wood and everything into a heap.

Outside Federica continued pumping the nearly fermented must in the old smaller fourth tank. She noticed that the juice in it was not bubbling with the same intensity as expected after two weeks. Federica returned to the winery intending to tell Anna she didn't like the lack of progress the batch was showing.

Anna was systematically smashing barrels and heaving the debris unceremoniously into piles. In two of the tunnels that had been carved into the hillside, there were still neat rows of sixty-gallon barrels of aging wine. But in the main workroom, Anna had destroyed almost all of the empty barrels. Just ragged heaps of wood staves, bands of steel, and a few untouched barrels remained. She was getting to those one at a time.

"Anna, what are you doing?"

She finished with another barrel before turning to face Federica. "Making certain we can't use any of these again."

"Father will be devastated."

Anna came down hard with the sledgehammer on another barrel top.

"Don't do that!" Federica tried to grab the hammer.

Anna pushed her away. "Stop interfering with things you know nothing about."

"I know you must have lost your mind."

"I'm just planning for our future." She attacked another barrel.

"I'm going after Father. You're out of control."

"You won't find him in the house."

"Where then?"

"He went to a grower's meeting up in Asti, as though talking to people who agree with him could somehow make better wine." She brought the sledge down on still another barrel.

Federica ran into Joseph's office. She telephoned her husband at home. No answer. She tried his office. The secretary said he left for a job. She said he was working at Schramsberg today and gave her the number for the winery. The person who answered said Scott was there and would send someone out to find him. All the while she heard Anna smashing barrels. Finally Scott came to the phone.

"What's up?"

"Scott, Anna has gone crazy!"

"Calm down, honey. Tell me what's happening."

"She's destroying our wine barrels. I'm afraid of what she might do next. I can't stop her. Will you come here, please?"

"I'm on my way."

In the twenty minutes that it took Scott to reach the *Immelhoff Winery*, Anna had completed her errant task. She set the sledgehammer down and leaned against a redwood vat to admire her morning's effort. She was a lot calmer than Federica.

Federica ran outside to wait for Scott to arrive.

"She's ruined everything! I couldn't make her stop. I tried. I really tried."

Scott gave her a hug. "Relax, honey. It can't be that bad. Let's go have a look."

They went inside. What they saw was bedlam. Barrel staves and metal hoops lay in scattered piles all over the concrete floor.

Anna smiled when she saw Scott. "Scott, do you want some wood? Just think of what an aromatic bonfire we could make with all this wine-stained wood. We might start a new tradition."

"What came over you, Anna?"

"Nothing came over me. I just made a decision."

"Not a very rational one."

"Did you come here to help me clean up or just to criticize?"

"Neither!"

Anna turned away from Scott. "Federica, will you see if Oscar is still out in the barn working on the tractor and ask him to come here? I could use a little help."

"No. I'm too upset to do anything for you right now."

"I can see that. Well, Scott, why don't you take your wife home? She won't be of much use here today."

He shook his head in disagreement. "I'll stick around here so long as Freddie needs me. As for you, Anna, what in the world are you going to tell your father?"

"Oh, I'll explain it to him."

Federica shook her head from side to side. "It won't be easy for him to accept this, you know?"

"No, nothing ever is." Anna remained calm. "In the long run, maybe he'll understand."

"Well," Federica said, "I will not leave here until Dad returns. I can't leave you alone to destroy the man."

"You're being overly dramatic. Barrels can be replaced."

"Dad has a commitment to this winery, too, you know? How can you be so inconsiderate?"

"Actually, I'm planning for our future. Sometimes you have to take drastic measures."

CHAPTER 5

Joseph, driving down from Asti, believed he had accomplished something in his meeting with the independent winemakers. The associates were quite surprised a few years earlier when Louis M. Martini actually sold his winery. But no one imagined Robert Mondavi would also follow that path, allowing Constellation Brands, a huge New York company, to acquire control of the entire operation, premium and luxury labels included.

Since then Robert Mondavi, the founder of the Mondavi Winery and the patriarch of the California winemakers, had passed on. Everyone was terribly concerned about how that would impact the industry. A lot of speculation and heavy discussion passed among the representatives. Most of them felt the sons would carry on, though they never showed the passion that had moved the founders. The meeting ended as had others with most members assured that California and the world still had a place for distinctive independent vinifyers. Joseph and the others vowed to support each other and stand fast in their endeavors not to let their guard down under pressure from the conglomerates.

Joseph felt good as he always did when he drove under the hand-carved *IMMELHOFF WINERY* sign and onto the beautiful property he was fortunate enough to have inherited.

Fretful about how her father would react to Anna's action, Federica refused to let her husband take her home, but she convinced him to go so he would be at home when their son returned from school. She then went into the house and slumped onto a sofa waiting for Joseph to return. When he walked in the house, she sat up and spoke to him before he had a chance to say anything. "Dad, are you going into the winery today?"

"Yes, honey, soon as I get changed. Why do you ask?"

"Well, there is a problem. I don't know how to prepare you for what you're about to find."

"Has the roof fallen in?"

"Not that, but I don't want you to be too shocked by what you are about to see."

"Now you have me worried. What happened?"

"Anna has gone on a rampage. I don't know whether she lost her mind or has become possessed."

"Is she ill?"

"Not in the physical sense, but you'll see what I mean."

"Let's go have a look." Joseph went through the house and out the back door with Federica following closely.

Anna had finished with her demolition so was by then attempting to stack the staves of wood and iron rings into some kind of order. She continued working even though she could see that her father had entered and was staggered by the destruction.

Joseph placed a hand against a redwood cask to keep from sagging to the floor. He spoke to Federica: "Do you know why she did this?"

"No, but I'm sure she'll have an explanation no one could possibly understand."

Anna stopped shifting the wood around. She looked at her father and stared straight at him with those dark penetrating eyes. "Do you like the beginning or the ending of things?"

"Don't start asking me questions. Just explain this!" He waved toward the destroyed barrels.

"It's hard to explain anything you will accept, but I'll try. I believe we need to redirect our efforts. These barrels are well past their prime. I've ordered some new ones to replace them. Any objections?"

"Are you crazy? We can't afford new barrels."

"I know you can't. I spoke with Stavos, the cooper. I'm buying new oak and paying for the cooperage myself, so you have no need to worry."

"Worry? I feel like I've been sabotaged. I can't believe you would undermine me this way."

"Don't make too much out of this. Some of these barrels have been around since before Prohibition."

"If you mean from the time of your great grandfather, Amerigo, you are wrong, of course. They have been replaced many times. But whatever he left for us, he was never destructive or inconsiderate."

"Don't fret too much about this. We still have plenty of these old barrels in the aging rooms. You can keep some of them for your memories, but eventually we should get rid of all those, too."

"Decisions like this are company matters. You don't just take a sledgehammer to your inheritance."

"I'll save what is good and shake off what is not. And I'll try not to lose any sleep wrestling with decisions."

"Anna," Federica spoke up in defense of her father, "I know you're bull-headed and think you are always right, but I never thought you had such a mean streak in you."

"It's not meanness, and neither of you seem to understand."

"You're right. I certainly don't." Federica went to her father, hugged him, turned, and unwilling to say anything more to her sister, left the winery.

Joseph looked over the devastation again, put both hands on his forehead and covered his eyes. He took a deep unsteady breath and turned his back to his impulsive daughter. Then, without expressing the depth of his feelings, he headed away from her out of the winery. Once outside, he stopped moving, confused, not certain what action he could take.

Finally he went into the house, showered slowly, letting the hot water massage his back. Afterward, for hours, he sat alone and thought. Anna didn't come into the house, so he had no idea where she had gone or what she was doing.

Situations like this certainly would have gone better for him, he thought, if the woman whom he had loved so much could have lived beyond giving birth to Anastasia. Raising two daughters and running a winery kept him totally occupied. But in times like this, he couldn't help wondering how much difference a good mother would have made in the development of the two girls. Federica at least had two years of her mother's influence, and she certainly developed vastly unlike Anastasia.

There was someone he might have called, a widow he respected and had known for several years; but no, he was far from ready to include someone else in family matters.

That evening, he had no interest in eating anything, though for some reason he drank a glass of well-aged Cabernet from the Bordeaux region of France before retiring to bed. Regardless of how hard he tried to suppress his anger and disappointment, sleep would not come to him.

During the night, he was certain he heard voices coming from Anna's section of the house. In fact, that was not the first time he'd heard such sounds. He could only imagine what his impetuous daughter was doing, but in the past he never questioned her about her private life. He feared now that she was capable of almost anything.

Without sleeping soundly, and feeling some of his world had collapsed, in the morning he staggered into the kitchen and brewed himself a cup of coffee. He attempted to read the morning paper. His mind would not focus on anything other than constantly reviewing and questioning why his daughter had taken such drastic irrational action.

Eventually Anna walked into the kitchen wrapped inside a terry-cloth robe, her hair a dark auburn mass of uncombed ruffles. She poured herself a cup of coffee and sat sipping it for a while before asking, "You still upset?"

"It goes much deeper than that."

"Really? How so?"

Joseph shook his head from side to side before he responded. "Don't ask me to explain myself."

Neither one said anything for a long period. Anna set the cup down but didn't stand up to leave. "I need a break from this pressure. None of my explanations seem to have any effect on any of you."

Joseph looked at her and then said, "Did you have a visitor last night?"

"My private life is none of your . . ." She didn't finish the statement. Instead she repeated his remark, "Don't ask me to explain myself."

"After what you've done, an explanation wouldn't mean much anyhow."

This time Anna stood up and started toward her rooms, quite relaxed in the way she moved. She paused and faced her father. "Dad, don't let a few broken barrels come between us. I didn't do any of that with a mean purpose as Freddie suggested. I hope you'll believe me." She then went to her father and kissed him, though he sat immune to her show of affection.

"Will you be taking out the Emma Mae Cabernet we now have aging in the old barrels?" he said.

"Why are asking me this?"

"I'll soon be taking the white Zinfandel from the second tank and having it lightly pressed, and I don't want you destroying those barrels."

She moved toward the door, but stopped again. "You're going to put white Zin in those old barrels?"

"Yes. I think a bit of oak would enhance the flavor."

"You are right about one thing: that wine is bland. A little oak would help, but I want to ask you now. Are you taking over all the winemaking duties?"

"No, but I can't trust you with everything. You can handle the Emma Mae Cabernet in the third tank and your Cab in the remaining old tank. I hope you will be careful with the Emma Mae Cabernet, our best wine by far. The white Zinfandel and the Chardonnay we left aging in the first tank will remain my responsibility. We need to hold onto something that pays the bills."

Anna almost accused him of being sarcastic, but for once in her life she held back and even decided to pay him a compliment. "Dad, I do like one thing that you have done. The three new tanks you bought are wonderful. We should be able to do good things using them."

"That's comforting to hear. And you are going to allow me control of the first two tanks?"

"Dad, let me explain myself. The white Zinfandel is yours no matter what. I won't tamper with it. Also I like the way you handle the Chardonnay, fermenting at a lower temperature and letting it ferment longer and not aging it in oak. I'm not entirely happy with it though, but that might be the result of the soil or climate here being not quite right for white wines."

"Keep going. What about the reds?"

"In one sense, we have a situation that works to our advantage. We are a small operation but we have survived through several generations. We are not unique but rare enough to develop a unique wine. I'm thankful you sent me to Davis where I learned the technical aspects of viticulture and enology. I wish I could have had a chance to study with that most famous winemaker, Andre Tchelitcheff. I've heard so many good things about his work. He was always most interested in quality over other concerns. He believed that the small operations which make one or two, no more than four varieties, have the best chance of producing a great wine.

"Of course, for any chance of success there should be one person in control. That is why I want to place myself in charge. I'm attempting, maybe foolishly, to use an old-world technique with the late harvest Cabernet. We'll see how that turns out. On the other hand, I believe I've done a good job handling the Emma Mae Cabernet. It's now a complex, satisfying wine. I want to go beyond that. Maybe try another variety. I don't know yet. I have to find a way for our combination of soil and climate to reach its potential so our little sector of land will produce an elegant wine of superb quality."

Joseph made no comment to show whether he agreed or disagreed with her motivation. He didn't argue or compliment but silently accepted what she had explained. He could have told her she still had a ways to go and that he had spoken with Tchelitcheff several times and believed the great man whom he admired probably would have taught her many of same techniques as he had. Instead they both looked away from one another, realizing they had gone about as far they could without another blowup.

Anna said, "I'm going to do something today I haven't done in a long time."

"What is that?"

"I've arranged an appointment to have my hair done at nine-thirty this morning."

"Oh! You shocked me there. I didn't know what to expect."

* * *

She was back in the lab at eleven and had hardly noticed what a nice job the hairstylist had done cutting and shaping her unusually thick, dark locks.

Unannounced and unexpected, Donald Stanton walked into the lab. Anna didn't acknowledge his presence.

"You're looking very beautiful today," he said. "What have you done?"

"I'm studying the influence of terroir in each of the five wine regions to determine which grapes will do best in this soil."

"I mean, what have you done with your hair? You look especially attractive."

"Why are you here?"

"Not to take you out to lunch. I don't need another lesson in humility."

"Get to the point. I'm busy."

"Something that Marco tried to tell you the other day, but you never gave him much of a chance. Didn't he mention that he and I might be going into a partnership?"

"Yes, but why would that interest me?"

"It would directly involve you. Wait!" He held up a hand. "Hear me out before you say anything. I think you might like this. A piece of property in the Carneros District has come on the market. There are numerous vines currently growing on the property and land for more planting. I don't know much about growing grapes, of course, but Marco certainly does. He says eventually he would like to quit traveling and become a full-time vineyardist, and maybe someday even become a winemaker."

"I don't see how any of this—"

"Wait. I'm still not finished. We're both realistic enough to know our limitations. We would like you to craft the wine for us."

"Where did you say this property was?"

Donald held back an enigmatic smile, knowing he had caught her interest. "Near Stanly Lane in Carneros. Marco says it's great for white wine grapes and Pinot Noir. The existing vines up there are Pinot Noir."

"Marco put you up to this, didn't he?"

"Well, it's not a conspiracy." Before she could object, Donald plunged into something he wanted to tell her. "Anna, there are some things about me I think you should know. First of all, I've only been in the Bay area a few months. My father was a banker, and I just kind of followed along. But my grandfather grew up here in Napa. He came to Southern California when it was time for him to attend a university. I often wondered why he never returned to such a beautiful place. Well, frankly, I've been fascinated by this wine business. So when the opportunity arose, I arranged to be transferred to San Francisco. I even asked to be assigned to the Pugliesi account."

"Why are you telling me all this?"

"I know you don't trust me. Since you won't allow me to take you out to dinner, I feel compelled to tell you a few things about myself so you can get to know me a little better. Don't you have any questions you'd like to ask me at all?"

"No. Why should I?"

"You are a tough case. Forget it. Let's drop my biography for now. I would like you to know that both Marco and I thought this land purchase we're considering could involve you in an important way. We were thinking this would be a good opportunity for you to try out some of your ideas."

"Isn't that a way of manipulating me? Marco knows I'm not happy with the Chardonnay we make here, and that I do want to try a Pinot Noir."

"Of course, he mentioned it, but it's not for manipulation. I don't know why you're so distrustful. We thought you might have some interest in our venture."

"I am interested in developing a better Chardonnay and making Pinot Noir."

"At least that's not a turndown. I'll keep you informed about our progress."

* * *

As soon as Donald left, Anna dialed Marco's office. She learned that he'd left that morning for Miami and wouldn't return for several days.

"Do you have a phone number where he can be reached?"

"I can give you his cell phone number."

"Won't do any good," Anna protested. "He leaves it turned off except when he wants to place a call."

"So I've heard," the thin-voiced secretary answered. "He doesn't want the phone to disturb other people."

"He's so considerate, he makes me angry."

"Pardon?" the secretary said.

"Never mind. Ask him to phone Anastasia if he checks in with you."

"Anastasia! Aren't you his ex?"

"Yes."

"Oh, he will be surprised to hear from you."

Anna shook her head and hung up just as Federica came rushing into the lab. "Anna, there's something going on, or really, I should say not going on with the fourth tank. I mentioned it to you before, but you were so busy smashing barrels I don't think you really heard me."

"I'm listening now."

"I'm only the cellar master, and I don't profess to know more about making wine than you, but I think there's something strange with that juice. It's hardly showing any chemical changes and doesn't give off the usual fermenting aroma. You should probably check it out."

"Of course. Let's go."

Once in the winery, Anna drained a sample from the tank, swirled and sniffed it, tasted a portion and then gave it a second tasting. A thoughtful look only lasted a few moments on her face until she realized the problem. "I was trying something with these grapes. The mold had some of the characteristics of the noble rot I had seen in France. I used an extract from the natural yeast as a starter, but I'm afraid that might not have been right for these grapes."

"Well, what's happening with it?"

"Not much that's good. I don't care for the direction this is going. It's not simply fermenting at all the way I had planned. Damn! Dad will have me on this one."

"What can we do about it?"

"First of all, I want you to remove the cap, scoop it out and set it aside in large plastic garbage cans. Maybe we'll try to rehydrate it. Apply sulfite to the remaining liquid in the tank. Tomorrow morning pitch in our proven yeast to start a new fermentation. In a couple of days we'll check it to find out what else we might need to do."

"Sounds promising. Is it going to be all right?"

"We'll know more in a few days. But I want to thank you for being alert, Freddie. This could have been a total disaster."

"Well, you have taught me a few essentials about making wine."

"Right now, as far as I'm concerned, you are the best cellar master in the world."

"That's a surprising compliment, Anna. Thank you. I think maybe we have saved it."

"For my sake and our winery's sake, I hope so, too."

* * *

Two days later before Federica got to work, Anna sampled the wine they had started in the fourth tank. She was not too happy with it, but detected a taste which might lead to something worth keeping. She figured she should give the new yeast a few more days to continue working on the remaining sugar. She also reasoned against rehydrating the remaining material from the cap. It contained too much tartaric acid and tannins from the grape skins. She decided to add it to the compost pile.

When Federica arrived, she saw her sister dumping the heavy residual pomace and remains of the cap with all its mold, stems and particles from the plastic garbage cans.

"What's going on?" she asked.

"We're not going to use any of this. I'm saving it for Oscar to use in the field. I want you to turn down the temperature on my experimental Cabernet, say about sixty-five degrees. I don't want it to ferment too quickly. This morning I detected a certain complexity which could possibly have some interesting results."

"Sounds as though you're not too sure."

Anna ignored her remark and then explained: "You know how much Dad likes to sell those white Zinfandels? Well, this might make a superior Cabernet Rosé. If it matures properly, it could be more satisfying than any of those pop wines he values."

"You haven't told Dad about any of this, have you?"

"I told him I was using an old-world technique. But it doesn't matter; he's still angry with me about the barrels. Let's wait a few days to see what happens."

"Anna, I'm worried. Why did you have to experiment with our livelihood?"

"Because I'm stubborn and refuse to allow our wines to be ordinary. Besides, we haven't lost anything—not yet anyhow."

"So, you don't think we'll lose the whole batch?"

"If so, I'll be the one to suffer."

"You see, Anna, that's where you're wrong. You're not in this alone. You already did incredible damage to Dad with your barrel escapade. Now this . . . this trial fiasco, noble experiment, or whatever the hell you call it, could demoralize our father."

"Don't be so negative. Dad's tough. He'll pull out of it."

"He should know what is happening with your so-called experiment." Federica did not wait for a response. She left Anna and went over to their barn to collect the bottles necessary to start bottling the previous year's Emma Mae Cabernet from the barrels as her father had asked. She decided not to check with Anna about her father's request.

When Anna saw her father come out of the house and head to the winery office, she called for him to come up near the steel tanks where she had finished unloading the plastic cans with the residual from her experiment.

"Before it's too late, Dad, I want to tell you that I have been experimenting with a natural yeast strain from the last harvest of Cabernet Sauvignon."

Joseph didn't say a thing but let Anna continue.

"I guess I should also apologize to Oscar because he was sure we could make a great wine with those grapes he worked so hard to grow and cultivate."

"Get to the point. What experiment are you talking about?"

"I detected some good qualities in the wild yeast and was sure I could develop a form of noble rot from the mold as they do in France. So I inoculated with my yeast. Well, Freddy noticed that the batch wasn't fermenting properly. She was right, so we removed the heavy cap and have restarted the batch with your German yeast. I kind of like what it's doing right now. Of course, it'll be a while before we know for sure."

"Have you finished with this explanation or apology—whatever it is?"

"Yes, for now."

Joseph was about to explode, but he kept his anger in check. "A sensible winemaker would have experimented with a limited amount. You have no limits to your recklessness. You risk a fourth of our harvest! How could you be so thoughtless?"

"Hold on now. Don't sell me out just yet. I'm not finished here. I have several ideas for the batch. As I said, it tasted fair this morning. It might become something special, something we might want to repeat in the future."

"That's also nonsense. Even if your noble rot experiment worked, you wouldn't have been able to duplicate the same strain the next year. The fungus doesn't repeat itself in the same way. You thought you could develop that overnight in your lab? The noble rot you referred to had taken the Europeans decades to perfect.

"Contrary to what you might think, you are not right all the time, and you are certainly not right this time. Just like your rampage on the barrels, you take action before you contact your brain."

Anna actually became subdued. She didn't attempt to say anything more than she already had. This time she accepted the criticism quietly and kept her defense to herself.

CHAPTER 6

While Marco was waiting in the Miami airport for his return flight, he called his home office in California. After he gave the secretary a brief rundown on his activities, she told him he had a call from his ex. He was not sure if that was good news or bad news.

Marco had fallen for Anastasia ever since he hit her with a rotten apple when they were in grade school, had been noticing her even before that. As they grew into their teens, they hit it off fairly well but always with an edge of uncertainty in their relationship. They began going together when Anna reached high school in St. Helena, dating one another but also other people. Marco wanted to go steady, but Anna thought that was juvenile. She thought they should either become engaged or continue as they were. Marco proposed, but she turned him down. Tying herself up with a fiancé before graduating from college was not for her. After she graduated from U.C. Davis, she finally accepted his proposal. They ran through a short engagement and soon married. Marco was extremely happy to have married the girl he had loved for so many years. Anna threw herself passionately into their marriage as she did most activities in her life. Sexually and intellectually, they were a great match. However, giving up her independence created no small amount of friction. Occasionally Marco mentioned that in a marriage both parties had to work things out. She countered by telling him that he could work things out all he wanted; she was happy with her life as it was. All-out warfare didn't begin until they had been married for over a year. The friction simmered for a couple of years without quite exploding. After two more years of strife and huge battles, they decided they were better off apart.

Marco was wondering if it was possible that Anna had called because she might want to get together again, but then he figured she wouldn't have phoned the office for anything as personal or important as that. As he sat there, he also wondered how long he could hold out for her, and how long he would remain with this job he was doing which was all right but certainly not anything he wanted to stay with all his working years.

Marco earned his knowledge of the vineyard at his father's side from the time he was a small boy until the year before he graduated from U.C. Berkeley when his father was forced out of his job.

Matt Preziano, Marco's father, had worked as a vineyardist in Napa until he took an early retirement, mainly to get away from an erratic, unreasonably demanding crop grower. The man would blame him for allowing the vines to stay exposed to too much rain, or not giving them enough water, even though they didn't have a sprinkler system. On frosty nights, he was accused of not using the burners properly. He didn't prevent the birds from eating grapes either, and did nothing about the wind. When the grapes were ripening in the fall, the elder Preziano supposedly left them on the vines too long, or he picked them too soon, thereby causing his farm to lose money by having to sell less than perfect grapes. In spite of all the real or imagined practices, Matt Preziano was an excellent vineyard manager who turned in many more good vintage crops than he ever did poor ones.

Through it all, Marco willingly helped his father, actually grew up with the crops and knew their behavior and requirements thoroughly. He learned how to trim the shoots and coax the vines into delivering their sweetest grapes. He loved the outdoors and was a natural in the field. He understood the grape's way and the wind's way, how the sun, the land, and the rain worked their wonders, and would have made an outstanding vineyard manager.

When the grower asked Marco to stay on as his vineyadist, Marco remembered the gruff man bellowing at his hardworking father far too many times. He looked right into the older man's eyes and said, "You never appreciated my father. I doubt you would appreciate me."

"But you are smarter than your father and much better educated. I was waiting for you to finish college, but now that he is leaving, the job is yours if you want it."

Marco smiled inwardly and answered, "I would never dishonor my father by taking his job."

"But he quit."

"No, he retired because you badgered him one time too many."

"You're leaving me on the spot. I'll be left with no one to run this place. I can't just go out and hire a good field manager without knowing what the man is capable of doing."

“You should have thought about that while you were forcing my father to leave.”

An avid reader, Marco continued with his studies at Berkeley where he received his degree in Business with a minor in Literature.

A flight attendant broke into his thoughts by announcing the first boarding of his non-stop flight to San Francisco International. As he boarded the 727, he had to wonder if he would be flying into a storm or if somehow the climate around Anastasia could for once be tranquil.

* * *

The climate around Napa in the late fall was serene, bucolic, and beautiful, though the sun was burning hot as usual for that time of year. In the afternoon, scattered white clouds carried by light breezes had moved in from the Bay keeping the temperature moderate.

Anna was sitting in her lab once again sampling the wine she had almost ruined. The results barely lifted her spirits. The German yeast they had pitched in did not work as well for a second or a malolactic fermentation as she had hoped. Even that wish quickly faded when she saw Marco’s pickup truck pulling up next to the winery.

Marco quickly walked into the lab, and attempted to greet Anna with a friendly hug. She simply put an open hand on his chest with light pressure to discourage the gesture.

“Haven’t you trained your secretary how not to react when I call your office?” she asked.

“I haven’t trained her, nor any woman for that matter. Why did you call?”

“Not for any romantic reason, I assure you.”

“I don’t doubt that for a moment,” Marco said. “Did you have a talk with Donald Stanton?”

“I did, and surprisingly enough he said something which interested me.”

She didn’t say anything more. Marco tried to wait for her to continue, but he was always uncomfortable when those long silences happened between them, as they often had between clashes during their marriage, so he took the initiative: “Look, I know what you talked about with Donald. We’d really like to know if you would care to come on board with us.”

"Coming on board sounds as if you mean riding along. I never just go along with others. Are you talking partnership, equal decision making, what?" she asked.

"All that has to be worked out."

"No. I have to know before I commit."

"Well, we haven't thought about asking you as a partner, unless you want to help finance the purchase. Either way, we want you to have complete control of all the winemaking."

"Then I would be just your employee. I don't need another job."

"I know, but you see, all that can be worked out if the project appeals to you."

"The project appeals to me, but I know you too well, and I find I don't know or care for your friend Donald Stanton very much at all. So I admit I have serious reservations."

"Let's take a drive up to Carneros, check out the property. I believe you'll like what you see there. Maybe later the three of us could get together somewhere for a business lunch."

"Give me the address. I'll meet you there tomorrow at two o'clock."

* * *

Marco had an offer from Scott to have dinner that evening with him, Freddie and their son Sandy. Rather than eating alone, as he had been lately, he accepted gladly. He had known Freddie and Scott since school days when he was a teammate with Scott on the football team, and he also really enjoyed talking with Sandy. The boy had a curious mind and was interested in so many things.

Sandy saw Marco parking his pickup so he ran out to bring him in.

"Hey, Sandy. Nice greeting."

"Come on inside. Everything's ready."

"You hungry?"

"Mom says I'm always hungry."

Freddie served an American-style dinner: steak, baked potatoes and a medley of steamed vegetables. Scott and Marco talked football. Both agreed that the San Francisco 49ers needed the likes of a Joe Montana or Steve Young to bring them back to greatness. After a serving of apple pie, they moved to the living room.

No wine was served at dinner, but Freddie brought in Cabernet for the adults and a Coke for Sandy.

"Why do you people always have to drink that wine?" Sandy asked. "Don't people in the valley ever drink beer or anything else?"

"That would be sacrilegious," Marco said.

"What do you mean?"

"Just kidding, of course. We're very lucky the culture of wine found a good home in the Valley."

"Found a home?" Sandy asked. "Where did it live before?"

"No one knows exactly where wine originated," Marco explained. "I have a theory that a long time ago someone saved a bunch of wild grapes in some kind of a container, a large jar maybe, so they could eat them later. Some of the grapes probably got crunched from the weight of the others. When the people returned to eat their grapes, they found them bubbling and giving off an interesting odor."

"That's from that moldy white stuff they get when they're ripe."

"That's right."

"You said 'a long time ago.' If it wasn't in Napa, where was it?"

"There were signs of wine being produced in Georgia about 8,000 years ago."

"Oh, Georgia! One of my classmates moved here from Georgia last year."

"No, Sandy, not the state of Georgia. The country is in the Caucasus Mountains near the Black Sea."

"Where is that?"

"Southeast Asia. Evidence of winemaking was also found in other sites south of there in Iran and Armenia about 7,000 years ago. They found traces of crushed grapes in Macedonia, and the Phoenicians distributed wine around the Mediterranean. We know for sure the Greeks used wine in ceremonies and had developed a screw-type press. The Romans did a lot to develop the cultivation and technology. They also used a wine press and were the first to make barrels for storing. Until then, wine was usually kept in clay jars called amphora with a layer of olive oil on top to keep the oxygen from getting to the wine and ruining it."

"I still don't see how it ever got here to Napa."

"Explorers brought grape seeds over and later vine cuttings to North America in the 1500s. It reached California in the 1700s when vineyards were planted at the missions."

"So now we're getting closer to home."

"Right, Sandy. Aren't you getting tired of hearing about all this history?"

"No. How come my teachers never tell us anything interesting about making wine and stuff?"

"Well, they have other information to give you. I'd like to tell you a story about how wine got started in an ancient country."

"Another story you made up?"

"Not this one. In Armenia there was a princess with a bad attitude. She angered her father, the king, so much that he didn't want her to be near him anymore.

"She knew she was in big trouble and believed life for her would not be worth living. So the princess thought she would end her life by drinking poison. She found some grapes in a jar that had spoiled. She drank all of the juice and it made her tipsy. She began to giggle and poke fun at people, made them laugh and feel good.

"The king saw how it affected people and declared that from then on they would make a lot more of that spoiled grape juice."

Marco had barely touched the wine in his glass while Scott had finished two. Freddie asked if either wanted more. They declined but Sandy held up an empty glass.

"How about some wine for me?"

"No."

"How about more Coke?"

"No," she said. "It's time for you to get ready for bed."

"Awww."

Scott pointed to the bedroom. "On your way."

Sandy went to his bedroom all right but not before thanking Marco with a high five.

* * *

The Carneros property was twenty acres of gentle rolling hills, still mostly green from earlier rains with patches now turning brown from the late autumn heat. A single row of trees bordered most of the section in question. Three wooden structures, a small barn for storage and two tool sheds, were located just off the highway. Even though the area was south of the Napa Valley proper, the air was cooled daily by the afternoon breezes wafting over from the San Francisco Bay and the ocean beyond.

About nine acres of Pinot Noir vines had been planted long ago but were now largely unattended. Anna shuttered at the neglected site. Marco saw that as a challenge. "I could get these vines in order long before the next growing season," he explained. "We might be able to start out with a good crop by next fall."

"What about the Chardonnay?" she asked.

"I thought maybe we could start with some good shoots from your own vineyard."

"Perhaps a few, but I'm not happy with most of ours. I do know where there are some choice cuts available from a vineyard in the higher elevation of our local mountains where they've had success making Chardonnay. I could purchase those as a starter."

"That's a great idea. See, I've known all along you're the one who could make the project go. Does this mean you will join us?"

"First I want to hear how you're going to finance this venture."

"Depends. Do you want a part interest in the project?"

Anna wasn't ready to answer that question, so Marco asked, "Would you be willing to sit down for dinner, the three of us, someplace nice where we can talk this over?"

"Sure," she said, thinking he would not agree if she chose someplace expensive. "How about Tra Vigna in St. Helena, and you two pick up the check?"

"That's a deal," Marco quickly agreed. "I'll contact Stanton and make the reservations for Saturday evening."

* * *

Donald Stanton was able to leave work early Saturday afternoon. He hurried to his apartment, showered and dressed with a more casual look than usual. A sport coat with an open shirt and matching slacks were about as casual as he could get and still feel comfortable. He managed to cross on the Oakland Bay Bridge before the traffic became unbearable. Staying with Highway 80, slowly making his way up through Vallejo, he drove on until he reached Highway 12 where he turned west. The road took him past the Carneros acreage he was considering, so he pulled over and studied the terrain for a while.

Wondering if he could turn part of the barn on the premises into living quarters, he realized he still had quite a bit of time before the dinner. So driving leisurely into St. Helena, he first located the restaurant where he would meet with his potential partners. Then he checked into a motel close by thinking he would not care to drive back that night, but also aware that he felt very good, even a bit relaxed in this rural atmosphere. No one knew better than Donald what stress his true intentions were doing to him.

He left the motel, arriving early at the restaurant. Several small parties were already under way, laughing, clinking glasses and saluting each other. Those groups were using the outdoor tables under the green leaves of an overhanging grape arbor. Donald went into the Cantina, a separate building on the grounds. He sat near a window and ordered a martini, looking out at the grounds, but he wasn't seeing anything out there. His mind was in high gear, figuring out how to finalize his plan before Marco and Anna arrived. When he saw Marco and Anna walking toward the restaurant, he left the Cantina to meet them at the arched stone entrance.

The threesome entered the main building, a brick structure that had been converted from a winery to a first-class restaurant. Two attractive girls, a tall blonde and a brunette with pretty hazel eyes, greeted them. The blonde said, "Welcome to Tra Vigna." When Donald saw the brunette with her long slender figure and willowy hair, and the most enchanting eyes, he became unusually quiet.

Marco responded for him. "I called for a reservation: Preziano for three."

The brunette smiled and led the trio to a table at the far side of the large dining room.

Donald followed the gently swaying figure and finally could think of something to say, "Would you like to join us for dinner?"

The girl's reaction was easy and genuine. "Wish I could, but I need to keep this job."

Donald had no fast comeback, so he nodded and sat at the table.

After the girl went back to her station, Anna spoke up, "You're really taken by that girl, aren't you?"

"I think I am. Somehow I'm going to have to talk with her before we leave."

"What about the blonde?" Marco asked.

"Very nice, but that brunette is the sort of girl I've been looking for."

"Never can tell unless you get to know her," Anna quipped.

"Before we leave here tonight, I plan to do just that."

The waiter, a young man with a neatly trimmed goatee, asked for their drink order. Marco was already familiar with the wines listed in a hefty leather-covered tome. He ordered an Altamura Sangiovese.

Anna looked at Marco. She didn't object but was curious as to why he would do that and not even consult her. She quickly went over the menu so he wouldn't order her dinner, too.

When the waiter brought the Sangiovese and deftly opened it, Marco deferred the tasting to Anastasia.

The waiter poured a small amount of the dark red liquid into her glass. She swirled it around to aerate the wine, studied the color against the glass, and then sniffed it before taking a nice long sip which she tasted thoughtfully while allowing the aroma to rise.

"Oh, no!"

"Is there something wrong with the wine, ma'am?"

Anna didn't respond immediately, but then said, "What a finish, long, smooth, full and satisfying. This is exactly the quality of wine I hope to turn out at my winery."

The waiter, very pleased with her response, asked her, "What winery is that, ma'am?"

"The *Immelhoff Winery*."

"Oh, I should have guessed. We stock some of your wines here. They are quite good."

"I didn't know you carried them."

"You can thank your friend here, Mr. Preziano, for that. He introduced them to us not too long ago."

"He is full of surprises, isn't he?" She looked disdainfully at her ex, but couldn't suppress a pleased smile.

Donald said, "Since Marco knows the restaurant, perhaps he should order for us."

"No," Anna objected. "Don't order for me. I know what I want. Bring me the Fusilli with Roasted Eggplant and the salad that matches up with it."

Marco said, "I'd like the Grilled Flank Steak with Roasted Peppers."

"That sounds right for me, too," Donald said. He kept both eyes on the receptionist each time she crossed the room leading other diners to their tables. However, he was quite able to concentrate when discussion got down to the important business matters they came to settle. He handled most of it, but showed he was willing to allow the others to have their say.

Anna started by taking advantage of the opportunity by quizzing him: "How did you learn about this property? I've checked, and it's not listed on any real estate offers."

"You're right," Donald explained. "The owner hasn't been physically able to work the land for a couple of years. His daughter now has the title that also carries a lean against the property. She can't pay it off and has informed my bank, which holds the mortgage, of her desire to sell. It's all legal. I advised her not to put it up for sale yet. I want to purchase it myself before some large distillery moves in. The question here seems to be, do you want to become a part of this?"

"I've already told Marco that I have no desire to be an employee," Anna said.

"We could go with three equal partners, or I'm willing to finance half if you two want to share the other half."

"No way!" Anna objected. "I'm not about to be subordinated to two men. What about you, Marco? Where do you stand on this?"

"I could accept being a third partner. I've been going over my savings, holdings and so forth. I believe I can handle the twenty percent down. I'd have to float a loan for the rest if some bank would carry it."

"You know I can arrange that," Donald said. "How about you, Anna? How are you financially?"

She knew that when she answered, this would be a commitment. "Okay, this is what I'll do. I'd rather own fifty-one percent, and let you two work for me; but I can't raise that much money. I can come up with twenty percent of one third. However, I will seek a loan from another bank. I refuse to have everything tied up in your one institution. Also, I must have one hundred percent of the winemaking decisions. That has to be written into the contract."

"Works out okay for me," Donald agreed, but then added, "I just wish you had more trust in me."

"I'm getting there, or I wouldn't have gone this far." She added, "Shall we have another bottle of Sangiovese? This one is on me."

The waiter brought the second bottle and filled their glasses. Marco raised his for a toast. "To a three-way partnership! Success and good days ahead!"

They all drank to the toast. Donald never let the inward smile show on his face that he covered by commenting on the pretty brunette hostess. "I wouldn't mind having a partnership with that one."

Marco shook his head. "Do you mean as a business partner or a bit more personal?"

"Well, I don't want to make any predictions. Right now I'm just waiting for an opportunity to introduce myself. Marco, you seem to know your way around here. Do you know her? Maybe you could introduce me?"

"No. Don't know her, can't help you there. You're on your own."

When the girl was finally standing alone, Donald walked over to her. "Hello. I've been wanting to talk with you."

"I thought so. I noticed you looking my way a number of times."

"I hope I wasn't staring."

"No. It's all right. My name is Courtney Gains." She extended her hand. "Yours?"

"Donald Stanton."

"Do you live here in the Valley?"

"San Francisco actually. But I'm preparing the way for a move here. Are you from this area?"

"My family moved here from Ohio," she explained, "but I only come down on weekends."

"Why is that?"

"I work Friday and Saturday evenings here at Tra Vigna. The rest of the week I go to U.C. Davis."

"Let me guess: enology?"

"No," she laughed. "Literature. I want to become a teacher."

"I imagine you'd be a good one. Would it be too forward if I asked to see you some time tomorrow?"

"I don't know. I spend most of Sunday studying, and then I leave Sunday evening for Davis."

"Are you a senior?"

"No." She had an easy laugh which only showed on the corners of her mouth and the sparkle in her eyes. "I'm only a sophomore."

"Well, even sophomores have to eat. Would you meet me somewhere for lunch?"

Just then a large party entered. Courtney turned her attention to them, got their names, but before leading them to their table outside, said, "See me before you leave."

Back at the table, Marco and Anna were in a serious discussion. They stopped as soon as Donald approached.

"How did that go?" Marco asked.

"Better than I had hoped. I think my future is right here in the Valley."

"Who was it said he didn't want to make predictions?" Anna needled him.

They finished the second bottle of wine, and called for the bill. Donald did manage to speak briefly with Courtney on the way out, just long enough to arrange to meet her at a little coffee shop she knew about off the main highway in Yountville. He nodded in agreement with that.

The three new partners drove away in three separate vehicles. That night, Anna received her visitor again. When the man knocked lightly on the door, she reluctantly opened it for him.

"I'm not sure I want to see you tonight." Instead of asking any questions, he waited for her to continue. "I have too much to think about," she protested. "Why don't you come visit me another time?"

"Of course, if that's what you want."

"It's what I want tonight. I'm really exhausted."

"You don't sound like the warrior woman I know: tough, armored, mobile, ready to battle anyone or anything."

"I have to build up my defenses," she said.

Instead of disputing her, the man nodded his acceptance and started to leave.

"Wait!" she said. "You may not know this, but when we are intimate and then you leave, something comes over me, and I get very depressed. I want you to understand, I have too much pressure on me right now to add your visit to my dilemma."

"No, I had no idea how you've been reacting to our relationship. Why do you think when I leave here, I have to sit out there in my vehicle to get myself back together before I can drive off?" He didn't expect an answer to that, but he knew what the answer to his next question would be. He had to ask it anyhow. "Why don't we just end this secrecy, let everyone know how we feel about each other, and stay together starting right now?"

She shook her head. "No, I have been married before as you know. I don't want another disaster."

The man knew when to stop pressing. "Fine. We'll talk about it another time."

* * *

In the morning Donald Stanton was up early. He wandered into the motel lobby where he poured himself coffee and ate a sweet roll while checking a street map of Rutherford. He didn't care about visiting the Veteran's Home, but he certainly wanted to have that lunch with the girl he'd met last night. After paying off his motel bill, and gathering his things, he drove northward directly to the *Immelhoff Winery*. Instead of going up the driveway, he pulled the car off the road and parked it just off the highway where it wouldn't be seen by anyone in any of the buildings on the property. Cautiously surveying the scene, he saw no one out of the house yet, so he walked quietly onto the grounds. As he meandered around, he looked through various windows into the winery and the workers' small cabins. He tried to swing open the big barn door, but found it was locked. He then strolled between the rows of planted vines, making himself feel right at home sampling a leftover grape here and there, letting his imagination do whatever it was doing.

Being alone on these cultivated grounds with the stone winery, the substantial house, the fermentation tanks, all the equipment, this experience helped him formulate plans that had been slowly simmering in his mental cauldron for several years. Working in a bank had always been for him a means to an end. Here on the grounds of an established winery, the feeling of what it would be like to take ownership of this piece of land and everything with it nearly overwhelmed him. He had to take in a deep breath and try to relax. Without doubt, Donald Stanton didn't want just a section of the development in Carneros. He wanted that and more, much more. He was also convinced there was something in his background which gave him that right.

CHAPTER 7

Anna didn't sleep well and was up preparing breakfast when her father came into the kitchen. "Like some French toast, Dad?"

"Sure, honey. You're up early."

"I have a lot on my mind. Yesterday I had a business meeting with Marco and Donald Stanton. Well, we decided to form a partnership to buy a parcel of land in the Carneros District. It's the old Wesley Vineyard, near Stanly Lane."

"I know the place. It hasn't been worked for several years."

"Right. Well, Wesley's daughter owns it now, and she wants a fast sale. Donald is handling the deal."

"The land has great potential. I'm not so sure about that Stanton fellow though. He comes up with some rather strange comments at times, as though he has another agenda on his mind."

"Has he ever been dishonest with you in any of your dealings with him?" Anna asked.

"No, not so far. I really can't fault him there."

"Good. I agree, though, he is kind of strange. Last night, he seemed straight enough. He understands financing, but he certainly has an eye out for the girls."

Joseph took a bite of the French toast and drank some coffee before responding. "Do you have any reservations about going into business with Marco? Your relationship there has not been exactly trouble-free."

"You're right about that; but whatever else I may think about Marco, I know I can absolutely trust him and he will be a good vineyardist."

"So with all that going through your mind, I can understand why you were having trouble sleeping. Do you want my approval on this?"

"No, I just wanted you to know. I'll make up my own mind on the matter. Those two men hooked me because they agreed to let me craft the wines, which I desperately want to do."

"How will that affect your interest and time here at Immelhoff?"

"Not at all. Most of my time will be still be here. We'll have to use the facilities here to make the wine. I love this winery. But with the Carneros' vintage, I'll be one hundred percent in charge."

"Will that make you happy?"

"Perhaps. I don't know. Maybe happiness is overrated. Maybe I'm just destined never to be happy."

Joseph looked through the kitchen window and was startled by what he saw. A man was out there sampling grapes from the vines that intertwined with the trellis his grandfather had long ago built out from one side of the venerable stone structure.

"Is that who I think it is?"

Anna looked out. "I'll be damned! That's Donald Stanton. What the hell is he doing here?" She started for the back door.

"Wait!" Joseph said. "Let me take care of this."

Anna started to object, but quickly decided this time maybe her father was right.

Joseph observed Donald for a few moments before going outside. He saw him pull at one of the few remaining bunches of grapes, but in doing so he nearly pulled the vine away from the trellis.

"Damn, he doesn't even know how to take a grape without destroying the vine."

Joseph caught himself wanting to rush outside, but deliberately slowed his pace, quietly closing the door behind him and walking up to the intruder who wasn't aware that he was close by.

"What are doing here?"

"Oh, Joseph, do you mind if I call you Joseph? I didn't know you were awake."

"Now that you know, please explain yourself."

"Well, I was just tasting a couple of these grapes. They're a little late in ripening, aren't they? Most of the other grapes have already been picked."

"What gives you the right to come on private property and help yourself to anything you want?"

"I thought since I'm responsible for your mortgage, I should know what's going on."

"We don't have a mortgage, just a loan for the refrigeration tanks."

"Same thing. It's a lien against the property."

"Is that a threat of some sort?"

"Certainly not. We should be able to work together. After all, we have something in common."

Joseph tied the vine back onto the trellis, holding back his temper, and then said to Stanton, "I think you better leave while I can still remain civil to you."

"Oh, certainly, I'll leave; but there's no reason to get upset. I do have a lot more I'd like to talk to you about, but perhaps this isn't the best time."

"Talk about what?"

"Like I said, this isn't the best time."

Joseph waited for an explanation, but Stanton just shrugged his shoulders and walked off.

Joseph watched Stanton until he left the property before going back inside the house. Before Anna could ask her father anything, he said, "Every time I talk with that man, I like him less and less."

"What did he say?"

"Not much; said he had more to talk about, but this wasn't the right time."

"He didn't explain his reason for being here?"

"Not to my satisfaction. He seems to think because we owe the bank money he has some entitlement to our place.

* * *

Donald Stanton really wasn't bothered much by being discovered snooping around the Pugliesi property. He thought he'd drive around the Valley for a while. When he saw the Sterling Vineyards, he parked his car and waited for the first tram ride up the hill to view the beautiful white-washed building like a Greek monastery crowning the hill allowing a spectacular view of the Valley. As he listened to the tour guide and later sipped their Sauvignon Blanc, his mind was busy plotting a course he might take to gain ownership of the *Immelhoff Winery* and perhaps one day even include another one as elaborate as this hilltop operation.

By noon he was sitting at one of the small tables near a window in one of the coffee shops at Yountville reading the paper while waiting for his date to arrive. He waved to the young waitress who came immediately to take his order, but asked her only for a cup of coffee.

Courtney showed up twenty minutes later than he expected. She parked her well-used Honda behind his BMW, and he noticed she carefully checked out his car. Casually dressed in jeans and a sweatshirt, she didn't appear to him quite as stunning as he remembered from the night before but still a very attractive young lady.

She came in and walked over to his table. He stood up intending to embrace her, but Courtney simply extended a hand. "Nice to see you, Donald."

"Call me Don."

"No, too informal. I don't know you well enough." She sat down and looked out at his car again. "Nice BWM. Yours?"

"Yes. Like it?"

"Of course, but I'll probably never be able to buy one of those."

"If you hooked up with the right people, you could have one quite easily."

"What do you mean by that?"

"If things were to go right between us, I would certainly be willing to buy one for you."

"Have I just been insulted?" she said. "Do you think I could care for someone because of an automobile?"

"It's been known to happen. A friend of mine used to say, 'Stick with me, baby; you'll be wearing diamonds.' "

"That friend sounds like a hustler. I certainly hope you're not like that."

"No, of course not, but I believe money can make a lot of difference in a friendship. Don't you think?"

"Money isn't that important to me."

"You might think it isn't now," he argued. "As you learn more about life, I'm sure you'll discover that it is."

"I think I just learned an important lesson. A friendship based on money can't mean a great deal. I believe you are much too sure of yourself and apparently quite insensitive about how others might feel." She pushed away from the table, stood up and calmly said, "I've heard enough. That's it for me." She headed for the door.

"What about lunch?"

"Hope you enjoy eating alone."

Donald watched her drive off and then ordered a tuna on rye, which he ate without feeling too terribly bad. In fact, he liked the coffee so well he asked the waitress where they bought it.

"It's an Italian brand," she explained, "from a distributor in San Francisco."

"Maybe you'd like to come along and show me where?"

The girl frowned and without answering walked away from the table and into the kitchen.

CHAPTER 8

Two of Oscar's teenage nephews were diligently hoeing weeds and trimming off a few of the more unruly canes from the untended Pinot Noir vines on the newly acquired Carneros property. The young men made a game of it moving parallel to each other, digging out row after row of unruly growth, hurrying, not quite racing but not falling behind either. By the second day, the field was showing a sense of linear order, encouraging the vineyards to return to their inherent beauty.

Anna was also at work clearing out a large designated section of neglected vines, trimming off the branches and excess growth so they could begin grafting the choice Chardonnay cuttings to the existing rootstock. While leaning into the work, she suddenly felt nauseated and then dizzy, which caused her to lose her balance and slowly sag down to the ground. Then, attempting to raise herself, she collapsed.

One of the field workers saw her go down. Both boys dropped what they were doing and ran to her.

Marco had just arrived with another truckload of the cuttings Anna had ordered when he saw her slump to the ground. He abandoned his pickup and rushed across the field to help her.

She resisted help from the two young men who got to her first.

When Marco reached Anna she was alert, but so obstinate she didn't want him to assist her getting up off the ground. "Don't be silly," she complained. "I'm all right."

Regardless, he helped her to her feet. "What happened?"

"I don't know. Maybe I tripped."

"No, ma'am," one of the boys explained, "you didn't trip. I saw you kind of just slip down to the ground."

"So I might have been a little light-headed," she countered.

"Thanks, fellas. I'll take care of her now. I'm glad you guys were here." They nodded their acceptance and returned to their work.

Marco looked at Anna and shook his head. "Too much wine, too much exercise can do that to a person, or in your case, too much work can destroy you. Like the Greeks, I believe people should use moderation in all things."

"Don't start on me with your antiquated nonsense. I'm okay now." She started to reach for another cutting, but instead grabbed for her midsection with painful cramps.

"I'm taking you to the emergency hospital."

"No. Not necessary. I have a doctor's appointment this afternoon."

"You do?"

"Yes. I've been feeling a little off lately. Maybe I have been over-doing it a bit."

"We're not waiting for this afternoon. Let's go see your doctor right now."

"No. There's no hurry. I know what the problem is." She thought carefully before she decided to explain, and then she spoke tentatively: "I think I might be pregnant."

"Let's go." Marco gently helped her into her vehicle and then drove the Cherokee to the doctor's office in the city of Napa. When she was finally in the examining room with the doctor, Marco phoned her father to tell him about Anna's condition.

Joseph dropped everything to hurry to the doctor's office as fast as the Highway 29 traffic would allow. When he arrived, Anna was out in the waiting room having a quiet conversation with Marco.

"Dad, you didn't have to come. I'm all right."

"What did the doctor say?"

"He said I haven't been taking care of myself, maybe overworking, and I do have a little high blood pressure."

"Marco said you thought you might be pregnant."

"Yes, just false signs. One should never try to analyze herself."

Marco added, "And the same person should not work two full-time jobs."

"I just wanted to make sure our new vineyards have an organic start."

"And you can't trust anyone but yourself."

"I bought the cuttings so it is my responsibility to give them a good start in life."

Joseph shook his head in disagreement and tried patiently to explain something to his daughter. "You do not have to do the vineyard work. We have one of the best field men in the business who is willing to bring his crew out to your vines. Also you should remember your ex-husband, this gentleman right here, your new partner, knows far more about growing grapes than you ever will. I thought he was to be the vineyardist."

"And you're about to tell me what I should do."

"Yes, just stick to the winery, Anna, and let those who know field work do the field work."

"So you are enjoying another chance to tell me off."

"Not really, only pointing out some realities to you."

"Well, Dad, you know something? I admit you are right this time."

Joseph put his head back and rolled his eyes to the ceiling. "Will wonders never cease?" He left, shaking his head in confusion.

Anna felt good enough to drive her own vehicle back to Carneros. On the way, Marco asked her an important question. "You might not like me to ask, but do you know who it was who almost made you pregnant?"

"How can you ask me that? You know as well I do who it was."

"I think I do, but you never acknowledge our relationship to any one, probably not even yourself. That kind of inaction is called denial."

"Now you're about to analyze me."

"No one could do that. I want to know how long we are going to keep up this charade. We sleep together, and during the day we keep up a running battle."

"Maybe that's why we broke up in the first place."

"If you had been pregnant, we would have had to let others know."

"Don't worry. Since I'm not, we don't have to tell anyone."

"No, but we do have to face each other and stop pretending we're not together when we really are."

Anna drove quietly for the rest of the way. Marco got out of her car and said, "I'll take care of clearing the vines for grafting. You should go home and get some rest."

"Will I see you later tonight?" she asked.

"No, not until you decide what our relationship is going to be."

"You mean unless I decide if we are going to live together as husband and wife?"

"You know how I feel about that, so it's up to you." He headed off to unload the cuttings from his truck but turned to say, "There is still an awesome amount of work to be done on this place. Even if Oscar can't come here, ask him if he will send over his two nephews. They are good workers. I'll be happy to teach them the proper way to trim the vines so they will produce the sweetest grapes. It'll be a skill they can use for years."

"And you will not spray any of these vines with pesticides?"

"I agreed we would go organic. Why do have to question everything I do?"

"Never mind. By the way, where is our partner in this enterprise? Shouldn't he try to be more involved?"

"Oh, I suppose he's in town manipulating investment accounts at the bank."

"I hope you're wrong about that. Do you think he's an honest person?" Anna asked.

Marco said, "If I didn't trust him, I wouldn't have gone into business with him."

"Well, I hope we're not both being naïve."

* * *

On the days when he was not busy with his job, Marco watered the Pinot Noir and worked on grafting the Chardonnay cuttings, though he had not had time to finish very many. The boys, brothers actually, were happy having steady work for awhile and became quite proficient with trimming the vines, but they were not allowed to do any grafting. Both sections of vineyard were looking better. Even the weather had been behaving.

Marco and Anna had gotten together again for nightly romances, but she still wouldn't allow him to go public with any explanation about their behavior.

"It's our business and no one else's," she would argue.

"And you are denying reality," he countered.

"I'm not denying you, so you better be careful not to tamper with our relationship."

* * *

A few days later, Marco and Anna were walking through their acres of Chardonnay and Pinot Noir, pleased that they had something to do with the direction these neglected fields were taking.

"All this is really quite amazing, isn't it?" Marco remarked. "I never thought we'd actually own a separate vineyard of our own."

"But do we actually own this one?" she questioned.

"What do you mean?"

"Well, I wonder what our partner is up to. Since we cleared escrow, he's never come out here to participate in any of the labor, nor has he converted the barn to the living quarters he said he would. There's just too much about him that I don't know and less that I trust."

"I have seen him in town several times," Marco explained. "He's busy with his responsibilities at the bank. Says he loves it out here in the Valley, but just can't pull himself away. One thing I don't like, though. He's all about money. He makes sure I never miss a payment, also said your father hasn't as yet paid for the new tanks."

"We have to sell the wine we're bottling from last year's vintage before we can start payment. He knows that."

"Let's not worry about him right now. It's far too beautiful here. You know what we ought to do? We should have that stag come here to spend some time in our new vineyards."

"You mean the white deer that came down a couple of years ago from the Mayacamas to forage at night."

"No, I don't mean that one," Marco said. "I'm referring to the legendary deer, the one that the Stags Leap district is named after. Haven't I ever told you the story?"

"Haven't had the pleasure. How does that apply here?" she asked.

"It was believed that a huge stag leaped into and out of the fields along the Silverado Trail. The vines responded by yielding the sweetest grapes of the season. My dad told me the old-timers looked forward to the visits, hoping the big fellow would eat some of their grapes so the rest would respond with sweet abundance.

"This continued until one day a farmer who didn't believe the story carried a rifle into his field. He hunted at night when the stag usually visited, but the deer was far too smart to be caught. When it saw him, it leaped away going from field to field until it found one where it no longer felt threatened.

"When the owner of that field noticed the missing grapes, he knew he'd have his best harvest ever and that the grapes would be in demand."

"That's romantic nonsense," Anna said. "The big deer probably chose the vineyards which already had the sweetest grapes."

"Not true," Marco countered. "Another grower tried to capture the deer, and that year his grapes were washed away by a flash flood."

"Enough of that. Time you finished trimming those Pinot Noir vines that were left here," she instructed.

"I'm far from finished with grafting the Chardonnay cuttings."

"We'll have to postpone that. We might even wait until springtime. The boys did a good job with the weeding. They are quick with the cutting, but they shouldn't be working alone out here. They need someone to watch over them until they gain enough experience. Where are they today? I can't ask Oscar to oversee this acreage. He has enough work just to keep Immelhoff operating. You should've been with them. I don't want the grapes growing under the leaves too close to the ground where they will mold. Since you know so much about vineyards, I'm surprised you haven't found time to do that part of the job yourself."

Instead of explaining how busy he had been, Marco said, "Thanks!" and rolled his eyes to the sky, holding back any sarcastic remarks he might have made. "I'll drop the grafting and get started with pruning this afternoon."

She nodded and got in her vehicle. Before driving off she said, "I'm going to call that silent partner of ours to find out what he's been doing. Somebody needs to light a fire under him, and I'm the one to do it."

Marco couldn't refrain from commenting, "You sure are a terror today. You scorched the boys and me, now you are going to burn Stanton. The Tasmanian Devil itself has no chance against you."

* * *

In spite of his outburst, Marco spent a pleasurable night with Anna. They never once discussed the disputes or friction that plagued them during the day. He left early in the morning as was his custom, but this time when he drove away he saw Federica driving toward the winery. He hoped she hadn't recognized his truck.

If she did, she had soon forgotten about it because of something she discovered that morning.

At the present time, all of the tanks contained wine in various stages of fermentation. The first run of the Chardonnay had been crushed and was ready to be moved to a redwood cask indoors to rest a while until they could find time for bottling. However, there was not enough oak for all of the young wine. Joseph's Zinfandel in tank two was being kept for storage with the temperature lowered to control the aging. The Emma Mae Cabernet was waiting in the third tank until the new barrels arrived. Anna's experimental late harvest Cabernet had finished whatever fermenting it was going to do and would be pressed and sent to the first tank as soon as that one had been emptied of the Chardonnay and cleaned thoroughly.

What Federica found was that all of the thermostats had been raised far above the marks she had set to control the action each tank required. She ran into the house where Anna was having coffee.

"Something terrible has happened."

"Calm down," Anna said. "What's wrong?"

"The wine! It's probably all been ruined. The thermometer on every tank has been set to max."

"What? That's terrible news. When did you last check?"

"Just before I left yesterday. Everything was fine. I can't understand how this could have happened."

"I'm not too concerned about my experimental stuff, but we can't lose the harvest we have in the other tanks. Are you sure you didn't make a mistake?"

Federica gave her sister a hard look. "The gauges have been adjusted since we finished the crush and fermentation. I don't change them; I just check on the temperature and the results every day. Why would I turn all four to max?"

"Of course, I know you wouldn't. That was inconsiderate of me."

"I can't believe you would say that," Federica said. "Where's Dad?"

"He went to some wine-tasting event in Modesto. Why are you asking about him at this time?"

Federica said, "Are you sure you didn't have something to do with this? Dad was so upset because of what you did to the barrels, this could ruin him."

"Wait a minute! You can't believe I would tamper with our wine?"

"I'm not sure what to believe." Federica paused before continuing because she knew she was toying with a tempest. She decided to say what she thought regardless of the consequences. "But who else has access to those tanks?"

Without answering, Anna pulled on a robe and rushed outside with Federica following closely. She checked all the temperature gauges. "They're all set correctly right now."

"Of course. I reset them before I came in the house."

"Okay then," Anna said. "Let's not panic. We'll test the wine. Maybe it's not too late."

Anna drew a sample of wine from all four tanks and poured each in separate glasses, slowly sniffing and tasting each sample twice with the same result each time. Without commenting, she handed the samples to Federica and watched for her reaction as she swirled and sniffed and then sipped from each glass.

Federica was not as sure about her tasting talent as Anna. She judged that what she had tasted seemed all right, except for the experimental batch, but said nothing and simply waited for Anna to state her opinion first.

Anna was so angry about the whole experience, at first she didn't want to say anything to ease Federica's concern.

Federica finally asked, "It's not too late, is it?"

No," Anna agreed. "If the gauges were changed during the night, they wouldn't have been on very long, and the weather was cool last night. There was probably not enough time to have influenced such large amounts of liquid." Anna narrowed her eyes and stared at Federica with still mounting fury.

"I guess we caught it in time," Federica said, gaining a little confidence.

Anna just glared, so Federica pushed a little: "Dad thought we should have moved the Emma Mae Cabernet to the redwood, but you wanted to wait for your new barrels. Too bad we didn't take his suggestion. This could've been a disaster. The Chardonnay and the Zinfandel he uses for his White Zin seemed all right. That concerns me because he says that wine earns us the steadiest income." She hesitated, but then decided to continue speaking her mind: "I don't know about your experimental Cab in the fourth tank. I didn't care for it at all."

"Don't worry about that. I'll take care of it."

"Well, what do you think about the others? Did they survive all right?"

Anna had to answer a direct question: "They passed the taste test. They seem to have come out fine, but I still can't fathom how you could let this happen in the first place. As cellar master, you are trusted with the future of this winery. I should have known better than to let you have so much responsibility."

"Are you still trying to accuse me of changing the gauges? If any one of us was involved, it was probably you. You're the one who wanted to take everything away from Dad so you could become sole owner of the winery."

"You couldn't be more wrong about that. I don't care to own the winery. Yes, I do want to control the winemaking, but I would never do anything to destroy our dad."

"You destroyed the barrels."

"That's an entirely different matter."

"Not really. It shows what you're capable of doing."

Anna drew in a deep breath before saying anything she would be sorry about later. "Those barrels were not worth saving. They had served their purpose and were ready for the junk heap. Dad was just too stubborn to see that. Those barrels did not contain our livelihood. Let me say this one time only, and you should believe me—I had nothing to do with changing those settings."

Federica also had to restrain herself. Her hands were shaking and her heart was running wild. "I want to believe you, and I suppose I believe you." She stopped and then added, "But why would you accuse me? I have nothing but love for you, our father, and this winery. It's in my blood as much as it is in yours."

Anna got herself back in control and spoke quietly to her sister, "I have to think this thing through. We should filter my Cabernet with bentonite to remove more unwanted elements. I don't care for the taste of it either. I have to admit I used poor judgment on that one.

"Right now I want to get dressed, and then I'll see you back in the lab. In the meantime, will you check again the progress of the Emma Mae wine? I wish Stavos would hurry up with our new barrels. I want to give that some time in the oak. A small winery like ours can't afford to lose any more product if we're going to stay in this precarious business.

"Federica, I'm sorry I accused you. I should know better. We shouldn't accuse each other. I still think you're the best cellar master anywhere around."

Federica both accepted and apologized by giving her sister a tentative hug.

* * *

When Joseph returned that afternoon, he brought the mail in with him. Among the ads and bills, he saw an envelope with the logo of the Pacific Central Bank on the cover. He opened that first and read a statement which said that payment was overdue on his loan for three refrigeration tanks; consequently, the loan must be recalled. "What the hell!" he said aloud.

Grabbing the phone he quickly dialed Donald Stanton's number. After punching one, and then four, and then three, he finally heard the man's recorded voice saying he was not available, and to leave a message. After doing that, he went out to the winery.

Both daughters saw him come in, stopped what they were doing, and looked at each other to see who would speak first.

"Something wrong?" he asked. "You girls look as though you've been frightened."

Anna said, "We came very close to having a disaster with our entire vintage."

"You mean you know about this message I received from the bank?" Joseph asked.

"What? No, I don't know anything about a message from the bank."

"Well, first tell me what is going on out here."

"We found that someone's been tampering with the wine. All of the gauges in the four tanks were raised far above our original setting."

Anna, with occasional comments from Federica, explained what they had found that morning and assured him that neither of them was responsible, but that they believed they had caught the problem before any of the wine was spoiled.

Joseph slumped down in a chair. "Read this." He handed the bank statement to Anna.

Instead of being depressed, Anna became suddenly very angry. "Your loan is being recalled! That Stanton bastard! I'll bet anything he's the one who messed with our temperature gauges."

"Why would he do something like that?"

Without answering her father, Anna said, "Let's go in the office." She led the way.

Inside she punched up Donald Stanton's number plus his extension and acually got him on the phone.

"What in hell are you trying to do by calling in my father's loan?"

"Just my job," Stanton replied, cold as a fish on ice.

"No way," she said. "We have an agreement with the bank."

"But," he countered, "I have been given control over this account. As I see it, no payments were ever made and I have no assurances that you will ever honor your responsibility, so I'm calling the loan."

"So that's what happened to the wine. You've been out here visiting our winery again, haven't you?"

"I don't know what you are talking about."

"Oh, you know all right. You raised the settings on our tanks knowing it would spoil the contents. Your motivation is so blatantly obvious. You were hoping my father would not be able to meet his obligation on the loan so you could seize control, but you couldn't wait for that to happen. So now you are calling in the loan."

"That's an absurd accusation. You're supposed to be the expert on making wine. What's the matter? Have you botched up your job, and now want to lay the blame on someone else?"

"Stanton, I didn't care for you from the beginning, but I had no idea you are such a slick bastard."

"A bastard? No. I know who my ancestors were. Can you say the same?"

Anna slammed the phone down in the cradle hoping the crash would damage Donald's eardrum. She started to storm out of the room, but stopped and addressed her father. "You know what he's attempting to do, don't you? It's not just punishing us. He hopes you will default on the loan and that he can take over our winery."

"Are you serious?"

"Yes. Why else would he tamper with the wine if he didn't want to destroy us? But there is more to this that I haven't told you."

Joseph took in a deep breath and exhaled slowly. "Don't you think this would be a good time to let me know?"

"A while ago, he suggested I should try to get you to buy more property and overextend yourself, and in that way I could then gain control of the winery. When I convinced him I had no such intentions, he probably decided he would try something else to acquire control for himself."

"Don't you think you should have let me in on such matters?"

"I haven't made it a secret that I want to run things here at the winery, but I promise I would never undermine you like that."

"I had no idea you were that determined. This has been a very tiring day." He sat back in his wobbly office chair, suddenly looking years older.

Federica hadn't been saying much, but thought perhaps it was time for her to help smooth out the roughness between her sister and father. "There has been a tug of war between you two; but, Dad, I know beneath it all Anastasia loves you. She would not take part in any scheme that would cause you to lose your inheritance."

"Thank you, Freddie," Anna said, and then turned to her father. "You are right, Dad. I want you to know I am on your side no matter what. Maybe I don't often let you know, but I do love you." She went to her father and hugged him around the shoulders.

Joseph accepted the affection, but was too disturbed to say much.

Even then Anna didn't hesitate coming up with a suggestion. "If I were you, Dad, I'd go to San Francisco and have a talk with the bank manager. See if you can save our winery. And while you're at it, make him understand he should fire that manipulating, cancerous employee if he wants to keep his bank in business."

Joseph agreed he would have a talk with the manager of the Pacific Central Bank, but at the moment he was drained of energy from the day's occurrences, especially after having driven to Modesto and coming back to such devastating news. He even confessed to Anna that what he had accomplished there was hardly worth the effort.

Federica dialed the bank number for her father. Joseph was able to arrange a meeting with the general manager at ten o'clock the next morning.

Federica decided to prepare a meal for everyone in her father's kitchen, so she called her husband to bring their son and join them for dinner that evening.

When Scott arrived and heard what happened to the tanks, the first thing he did was call the local sheriff's office to arrange for someone he knew to come over to investigate the grounds for any clues which might have been left by an intruder.

Anna thanked him and they sat down for one of Federica's simple but great dinners: pasta baked with ricotta, peperonata and plenty of Joseph's good Emma Mae Cabernet. They even let Sandy take a few sips of the wine this time.

CHAPTER 9

Starting out early in the morning, Joseph decided he would drive the Sears Point road to San Rafael and south from there over the Golden Gate to get into the city. He dreaded the traffic he would find but, since the last earthquake, was weary of the route via Richmond and over the Oakland Bridge.

As it turned out, he enjoyed the drive more than he expected. On his left he had a clear view of San Pablo Bay while skirting along the marshes on his right. He counted two herons and three egrets plus a score of mallards and a graceful white crane gliding in for a landing on the wetlands. Then he encountered the work traffic approaching the Golden Gate. It was heavy as expected but somehow moved steadily southward.

He squeezed his Lincoln into a small nearby parking lot. Walking into the bank, Joseph saw Stanton sitting in his glassed-in office. Stanton gave him a weird smile and started to stand up, but Joseph walked by without even acknowledging the man.

Arbuthnot, the manager, shook Joseph's hand and welcomed him into his office. "Have not seen you for quite a while, Mr.Pugliesi. How are things going?"

"Not well at all. The reason I haven't seen you is that you turned over my account to Donald Stanton. I've been having to deal with him."

"Yes, he's an aggressive young man always on the lookout for opportunities. Is there a problem?"

"Certainly is. Do you know about this?"

He handed Stanton's letter to Arbuthnot who took his time reading it carefully, and when he finished without commenting made one quick negative shake of his head.

"Didn't he consult you about this?" Joseph asked.

"No, sir. This is news to me."

"In our agreement, there were to be no payments for the loan until we started realizing income from last year's bottling."

"Yes. I remember the circumstances."

"What does this mean? Will you be taking back the refrigeration tanks? Is that even sensible?"

"Well, it certainly is not a financially practical solution. Apparently Mr. Stanton doesn't realize what is involved here. We can't take back three already installed stainless steel tanks like repossessing automobiles. Their removal, transportation, storage, and depreciation would be unreasonable action. Something else has to be worked out."

"We had to use *Immelhoff Winery* for collateral. Is this now an attempt to confiscate my winery?"

"That is certainly not my position or Pacific Central's."

"My daughter believes your employee, Stanton, is hoping that we will default and thereby lose the winery, and that somehow he will become the beneficiary."

"That would not happen. Matters like this must be reviewed by the board before any action can be taken."

"Call him in, and we'll discuss it."

"No. I won't humiliate my employees that way, but he and I shall have a head to head. I will let you know what transpires."

"I hope you don't mind if I have a few words with the man before I leave?" Without waiting for an answer, Joseph turned and strode over to the glass door.

Donald stood up as Joseph pushed the door open. "I thought you might stop by to see me."

"Isn't that perceptive of you? Maybe you'd like to explain what you think you're doing?"

"Just my job, of course. Sit down and let's be civil about this."

"Don't talk to me about being civil. Do you consider this justifiable?" He threw the letter on the desk.

"I simply took an independent action."

"Taking independent action is often rewarded, but, no, what you are attempting is bordering on the criminal."

"Recalling a loan is not criminal."

"No. However, entering private property and tampering with the equipment certainly is."

"Mr. Pugliesi, I don't believe you know what's involved here."

"Well, we have a detective investigating the winery this morning. If we find you had anything to do with the tampering of our wine, we won't hesitate filing charges."

"I don't suppose you would. But hold on a minute. What I mean by being involved has to do with family history."

Joseph sat back and stared with controlled anger at Stanton.

And so Stanton thought it was time he explained himself. "Mr. Pugliesi," he said with a lot of sarcasm in his tone, "a while ago, I tried to talk to you about me, or maybe I should say about us, but you showed no interest at all in what I had to say."

Joseph didn't respond. He just waited for Stanton to continue.

"Do you know much about your background? Your ancestry, I mean?"

Joseph continued glaring, so Stanton went on, "You use the name Pugliesi, but that was not your father's name. You were born out of wedlock, raised by your mother and later a stepfather. Do you even know the name of your real father?"

"Why is that any of your concern?"

"I'm about to tell you. You and my father were half-brothers. Your father and my grandfather were the same person. Stanton was his name. Your real name should have been Stanton, but your mother was too stubborn for that. She not only refused to marry my grandfather, she sent him away. When you were born, she chose to name you Pugliesi."

Joseph was not entirely surprised because he knew a little about his mother. But he was stunned to learn that this tyrant-in-training could be related to him. He sat quietly thinking about what this information meant and what Stanton must have been planning. He decided to question him about that. "I'm not disputing anything you've said because you are probably right with the circumstances but not about why my mother didn't want to marry the man who got her pregnant. That was a youthful, wartime mistake. So, knowing what you do about your background, do you actually think that gives you some kind of rights to the winery?"

"You're damn right it does. I didn't get this bank job by accident. I planned this move to Northern California and made sure I got the Pugliesi account after I was hired. You see, I suspected there was a good reason my why grandfather left this beautiful Valley to settle in Los Angeles. When I looked into the matter, I discovered his connection here and that I rightly should have inherited a share of the *Immelhoff Winery*."

"I don't follow your reasoning. The man was never a part of our family or this winery. I told you that what happened with my mother was a wartime romance."

"He was still my grandfather. Therefore you are my uncle. Anna is my cousin."

"All that started on the male side, but you have no bloodline from anyone in the Pugliesi family."

"Maybe not, but I should have."

"That's preposterous. If they had married, you wouldn't be the same person you are today. You might not have been born, or who knows what the results would have been."

"The fact is that I am here, and I have this connection. I could have been the one to inherit the winery instead of you."

"Ridiculous! If this is why you have been tampering with our harvest and attempting to recall our loan, you're way off base."

"I haven't admitted to messing with anyone's wine, and no matter what Arbuthnot might have told you, he will back my request to call in your loan. I'm sure he would be happy for the bank to own a winery. I would be first in line to assume the payments and thereby gain my inheritance. It's no problem for me to get a loan." A smug, nervous smile drifted across his face and soon faded.

Joseph rose quickly from his chair. "You're sick, you know. You definitely need help."

"You're not getting away with what should have been mine," Stanton countered.

"You really do have your brain connections all messed up. You're not even a shirttail relative."

Joseph left the bank in an angry mood that became solemn by the time he returned to his car. He drove back over the Golden Gate Bridge. After crossing the span, he didn't stay on Highway 101. Instead he turned onto the Sausalito off-ramp. The road curved around and led him down via Second Street into town. He remembered that his great grandmother, the original Anastasia, had once owned an Italian restaurant here. If he could find it, he wanted to have lunch in the same place to feel a connection to his past and think over what had just occurred.

The restaurant was still there on Bridgeway, just north of Spinnaker Drive. He managed to park three blocks north and walked back through the village, now a crowded tourist destination. The restaurant had changed owners several times. Joseph didn't care. He wanted to have lunch there so he could reminisce and get his thoughts back in control. Donald Stanton had upset him so that he felt unnerved, almost brought him back to the uncertain days when, as a young man, he had wandered around San Francisco trying to decide what he would do with his life. But this was different. Now he had to figure how to continue without having everything he had worked for completely disrupted by some disturbed person. He also wondered how Anna would react to the news he had just received about her newly acquired cousin.

The restaurant was now not much more than a fast-food place like those found in numerous shopping malls. Joseph ordered and paid for the food at the counter, then found a plastic chair at a small table and waited for his order.

The sauce they used was poured directly from a large commercial container, heated but not enhanced with garlic, onions, or any spices. They heaped the thick red paste on the pasta he had ordered and served it to him with a hunk of greasy bread which was their idea of focaccia.

He could barely manage to eat a few bites and had no chance to concentrate on what actions he might take to improve his financial situation. All he could think about was that this was the most unsatisfying meal he had ever tried. He pushed the plate away and walked out. The experience left him feeling worse than he had when he went into the pseudo-ethnic restaurant.

* * *

During the morning when Joseph had driven to Pacific Central Bank, Anna called Marco to tell him what Donald Stanton was attempting to do about the loan and what she suspected he might try to do with their current joint investment.

"What do you think we ought to do about all this?" he asked.

"I know what I'm going to do. As soon as I hang up, I'm heading to my bank in Calistoga to withdraw my interest from the Carneros property. I didn't trust that creep from the beginning, so before I went into a partnership with him, I included my own option to pull out. Then I think you should meet me at the property. We need to take back our Chardonnay vines before that vermin cheats us out of everything."

"We can't pull out the vines. That would take forever."

"We can certainly cut off the shoots we grafted. I don't want to leave that bastard anything of ours."

Marco reluctantly said, "Okay, I'll see you at the property, but I think you're being hasty."

"This is not the time to be timid. We're working with a snake. I want to get out before he strikes again."

Marco was at the property long before Anna arrived. However, he hadn't done a thing about recovering any of their shoots. He walked up and down the rows of vines looking at the plants they had altered, noting that the grafting was taking hold. He couldn't force himself to cut away the new growth he and Anna had started.

"What are you waiting for?" she asked when she jumped out of her Cherokee. "I thought your truck bed would be full by now. I've already figured what we can do with the cuttings. We can clear the upper section of the Emma Mae Vineyard and next spring plant them in that soil. I believe these cuttings would blend well with our already planted Chardonnay."

"Oh, Anna, I just don't have the heart to destroy these vines. We don't know for sure what Stanton will do about this property. Whatever he's trying to do to the *Immelhoff Winery*, it has nothing to do with this project."

"Have you talked with him yet?"

"No."

"All you can be sure about him is that he is as deceptive as hell is hot. He talked so big about converting the storage building here into living quarters. Has he done anything about that or helped us with one single vine on this land?"

"Well, he's been busy at the bank. Besides he's just not a field worker."

"I don't know about you, but I'm not waiting. We have to salvage something from this operation." Anna grabbed a clipper and sliced off a cutting just above the graft. She did another and another.

Marco shook his head and reluctantly started on the next row. In about two hours they had his truck bed filled with cuttings, and then let the tailgate down on her SUV and began filling that with more cuttings. When both vehicles were loaded, they drove immediately to the *Immelhoff Winery* and unloaded the cuttings, stacking them against a wall inside the old barn.

In the kitchen, they threw together a late lunch and were soon on their way back to Carneros to retrieve more of their vines.

Marco followed Anna off the highway and up the dirt trail to the large storage building.

Stanton's black BMW was parked in the shade with him leaning against a front fender. He was more than a little upset about what he saw had been done to the Chardonnay vines. He directed his anger to Anna. "I suspected something was wrong when your bank notified me that you have pulled out of our partnership." He made a vague gesture toward the vines that had been stripped. "Now what in hell have you been doing to my vineyard?"

"Protecting what is ours."

"None of this is yours. You are trespassing on private property."

"What are you talking about?" Without waiting for an answer, Anna went on, "I don't know how I could have been so foolish as to go into business with you." She turned away from him and headed for the nearest row of uncut vines.

"Hold on now. You relinquished your interest here when you pulled out."

"So what! Marco still retains his interest in this fool's venture."

"I wouldn't be so sure about that."

"Meaning what?" she snapped at him.

"Meaning I've decided to take control of Marco's third. After all, look what he's doing. He's been helping you without consulting me."

"Wait a minute!" Marco cut in. "What do you mean, you are taking control of my third?"

"It's apparent to me that I can't trust either of you, so I'm releasing you from the partnership."

"You can't do that."

"Oh, but I can. I wrote it into the contract. I have an option to buy you out any time I please."

"You said that was put in to allow me to feel safe about the investment in case I couldn't keep up with the payments."

"Certainly, but it was also my choice whether to exercise the option."

Anna was by then super furious with Stanton. "You get worse by the minute. What about the payments Marco has already made? You can't walk off with his principle."

"No, I won't do that. I respect Marco. In time I'll return his money, and then I'll own one hundred per cent of this Carneros property."

"I've heard of predatory loan sharks. You are that and worse."

"No, Anna, my reasons are much more personal than you know."

"You are so naïve. With no knowledge of winemaking, you'll fail like the miserable creature you are."

"What you're saying doesn't mean a thing. Land is always valuable. I arranged this purchase at a bargain price. I'm sure I can more than recoup my investment any time I want."

"Listen, Donald," Marco tried to keep his voice on an even tempo, "if that's true, since you won't be making wine here, why don't you let us have the rest of the Chardonnay? Actually, the shoots are rightfully ours. We bought them independently and grafted them ourselves."

"Now you're pushing your luck, Marco. Just get the hell off my land."

"That's how you want to treat our friendship?"

"Right! Take that woman of yours, ex-wife, courtesan, or whatever she is," he said with a sneer, "and leave."

Marco moved close to Stanton and pointed a finger in his face. "Be careful how you address her. I'll take your head off if you utter another insulting word."

She placed a hand on Marco's shoulder. "Let it go, Marco. He's not worth it."

"The thing I can't understand," Stanton addressed Anna, "is why Marco has stayed with you." He glared at Anna, but didn't dare insult her with Marco appearing ready to strike him. "Another thing," he said smiling as though he had some inside knowledge, "you two are closer than you're letting anyone know."

"Whatever we do is none of your affair," Anna said.

"Maybe not, but I know a lot more about your affair than you are willing to admit. I have checked public records regarding your marriage and would-be divorce. Anna, you are a fraud, and so is Marco for that matter."

Marco had been holding back and restraining himself, but now he thrust himself between Stanton and Anna and jabbed a finger into his face. "Mister, you have pushed this too far."

"Maybe so, but I want you two to get off my land." He stepped away from Marco and addressed Anna, "I'll come by later to pick up the cuttings you have stolen."

"If you step anywhere onto our property again," Anna said in a low controlled voice, "you'll regret it."

"Perhaps not. Have you talked with your father since he left my office this morning?"

"No. What you are insinuating now?"

"Talk with him. You'll find out."

* * *

That evening when Anna sat down with her father, she felt compelled to relate the events of her day. "That Donald Stanton really cut himself off from us this time."

Without even listening to what she was going to say, Joseph, who was upset himself said, "Maybe not. You have to know. He thinks he is a member of this family."

"What are you talking about?"

"I don't mean to shock you, but he has proof that my father and his grandfather were the same man. The man's last name was Stanton. I knew my mother never married the one who got her pregnant, but I never thought much about those matters since I was a kid. Now I feel nauseated ever since I realized he might be right about our relationship. But also—and this is where he is way off base—by some twisted reasoning, he believes he should have inherited this winery."

"So that's why he's been doing all this manipulating. He certainly has a bizarre way of intruding himself into our affairs. You know he not only tried to recall your loan, I have no doubt he was the one who tampered with our fermentation tanks, hoping to push us into a financial bind. Today, after he found out I withdrew my investment from the Carneros' contract, he threw Marco out of the partnership so he could grab it all for himself."

Joseph frowned but didn't respond to that bit of news. "Do you realize," Joseph asked, "that Donald Stanton is your cousin?"

Anna took the information quietly, but she began seething inside. "Now you're making me nauseous." She shook her head to chase away the thoughts. Then, as she was often able to do, she quickly accepted the situation and began looking for a solution. "Well, I guess most families have to carry some sort of burden. What can we do to keep him out of our lives?"

"He has some sick idea that he is going to seize control of it all," Joseph said. "I am afraid the bank manager, that sluggish Arbuthnot, will not try to stop him."

Anna's brain was really working by then. "But if we were to start payments straight away on the loan, he wouldn't succeed. Is that correct?"

"That's right. However, I don't have ready cash, and I won't take on a second mortgage. What do you have in mind?"

"I'll use the money I withdrew from our stupid joint venture to start monthly payments on the loan. That should carry us until we can get some cash flow from last year's harvest."

"You would do that?"

"Of course, I would. We can't have that creep take away our means of living, our way of life."

Joseph walked up to his daughter, drew her toward him, and gave her a long overdue hug.

She said no words, but was more pleased than she would admit even to herself.

"I better have a talk with Marco," she said. "If he is so good in public relations and sales, we also need to see more results from his efforts."

When Anna reached Marco on his home phone, he said he would love to have dinner with her. Instead of going out, he suggested that she should come over to his place tomorrow evening. He would prepare dinner so they could have a talk, because there was something important she should hear involving both of them.

CHAPTER 10

Late in the afternoon Scott and Federica were waiting for their son to come home from school. When he didn't return, they called his friends Billie and Jasper. Neither one had any idea where Sandy was. They then called the local police who posted an alert call to all patrol cars.

About seven o'clock both parents heard bicycle tires sliding on the gravel outside. Sandy tentatively walked into the house. When Scott and Federica saw him, they didn't attempt to hide their alarm at his appearance. His head had been shaved up both sides, leaving a two-inch-wide purple Mohawk crowning the top of his young head.

Sandy tried to explain to his parents: "I would have come home sooner, but I had to ride all the way down to Napa City. There's a guy there who does hairstyling for rock bands. How do you like it?"

"Before I comment on that," Federica said, "I want to know why you couldn't call home to let us know where you were and that you were all right."

"I was all right."

"But we're not mind readers! How were we supposed to know?"

He remained quiet for a while before he explained, "I guess I knew if I told you, you probably wouldn't have let me go."

"You're right about that. As for what I think about your lovely hairstyle, I just have one question. Did you ever see a Mohawk Indian with purple hair?"

"Awww . . . It's not that bad."

Scott was partly amused but at the same time angry. He let himself soak it all in before he finally spoke up. "I think perhaps you were not at all sure you should have gone through with what you just did."

"What do you mean?"

"We talked with your two best friends. They had no idea where you were or what you were having done to yourself."

"You called Billie and Jasper?"

"That's right. Were you afraid to tell them about your plan?"

"No way. I just wanted to surprise them."

Federica cut in, "To be the first in your block to show that you have lost your mind."

"C'mon now. It's not all that bad."

"Hope you like leftovers," she said. "Then you will take a shower and go to bed. I hope your hair doesn't stain the pillows."

"It's fast color. It won't fade or anything."

"Great! Is that the good news?"

"No. At least I didn't get a tattoo or have my nose pierced."

"We have so much to be thankful for. Follow me."

She led him to the kitchen table where he sat and attacked the still-warm leftovers.

* * *

After school the following day, Sandy rode his bike to the *Immelhoff Winery*. He saw his mother working outside with a girl who looked like an older teenager. She was kind of cute, a little old he thought, but he really had no time for girls just now. He waved to his mother, but didn't want to talk with her in case he would have to explain why he was there.

Going into Anna's lab, he looked around with some interest at the technical things on her worktable and the various flasks and tools shelved on the walls. "You use all these gadgets?" he asked her.

"Yes. Do you want to learn how?"

"Naw. I don't care about making wine. Not supposed to drink it anyhow, except when Dad lets me take a sip so I know what it's like and maybe won't go out drinking on my own."

"I see. Well, what can I do for you?"

"I want to talk to Grandpa. Is he around?"

"He's inside the house. I think maybe in the kitchen."

Sandy heard her but didn't make a move toward the house. He stood watching Anna for a while. She didn't say anything to him so he asked her, "Aren't you going to say something about my hair? Everyone else does."

"No. What you have outside your head doesn't interest me. It's what's inside that matters."

"Is that a put-down?"

"Not meant to be. I guess we'll just have to wait to find out what comes out of your head besides that growth you've sprouted."

"Boy, you're tough. I think I'll go find Gramps."

* * *

Joseph saw his grandson come in, and immediately set down the knife he was using to dice garlic. He poured a glass of milk for Sandy and gave him some graham crackers, which Sandy accepted and ate without slowing down.

Between crackers he said, "You told me one time I could come to talk with you any time I wanted."

"Of course. The offer still holds."

"Well, it's not about my hair."

"I hope not."

Sandy grimaced but thought he'd better let that one go. "I want someone who has enough authority around here to take me out of school. The classes are too long, and the teachers are boring."

"Do you want to go to another school? I might be able to arrange for that."

"No! I think I'm just wasting my time in school. I feel like I'm just sitting there, a nothing, a no one. I'd rather get a job and go to work."

"There's something here you don't quite understand. You already have a job. Being a student is your job. You're not a nothing. You are a student. That is what you are, your identity, and it's a very good one to have."

Sandy squirmed and raised his shoulders as though carrying a burden. "But I'm not a good student. I don't like being in school at all."

Joseph realized he needed to be patient with this youngster, so he didn't rush his speech. Using a moderate, understanding tone, he said, "You are unhappy because you're fighting it. If you could accept the role and for now try being the best student you could be, the time will pass quicker. Eventually you will graduate, you will become other than a student, and then, of course, you'll still have to become the best you can be in whatever you choose."

"Like Aunt Anna?"

"Exactly! She's one of the very best at what she does."

"But I don't want to be a winemaker."

"You don't have to be, and you don't have to choose right now. Just know that no one will force you into doing anything you don't want."

There was something else Sandy wanted to say. He wasn't sure he should ask about it at this time, but he thought he might as well take a chance. "I read something in a magazine about this guy who takes pictures of foreign cars, you know, sports cars and like that."

"You want to work with cars?"

"No, not that. I want a camera, so I can take pictures of cars and things." Joseph really seemed to be listening, so Sandy went on, "Mom and Dad are kind of angry with me right now. They gave me a nice bike, but I rode it all the way down to Napa City, came home real late and got into big trouble with my hair and all, you know?"

"You don't blame them. Do you?"

"I guess not, but if I ask them for a camera now, they'll just turn me down."

"Tell you what I'll do. If you work on your attitude toward school, by that I mean, don't think about it as one boring class following another, but try to get interested in the subject the teachers are discussing and the assignments they give you. See if you can find something you might like about each subject. I know the time will go faster if you're not just sitting there staring at the wood grain on the desktop. If you show some real improvement, I promise I'll see what I can do about getting you a good camera. How about one of the new digital ones?"

"That'd be great. I could print my own pictures."

"Right! You know even photographers have to be students."

"Wait a minute now! I didn't say I want to be a photographer."

Joseph had to smile at his grandson's quick defensive stand. "You never know," he countered.

"No way. I just want the camera to be like a hobby."

"Perhaps you know yourself better than anyone thought."

Sandy shook his head but still gave his grandfather a big thank-you hug before he went outside.

He saw his mother and her pretty helper trimming the overgrowing vines from the trellis that had been built out from the side of the winery. "Hi, Mom," he shouted without slowing down. "I'll see you at home later." He jumped on his bike and sped off before Federica could ask him a bunch of questions or maybe even introduce him to that girl.

* * *

Anna knew all along that Marco was a good cook, but the evening turned out to be far more than she expected. When she first stepped into the house where she and Marco had lived, she was almost overwhelmed with nostalgia from those married years. Not much had changed inside the house. He'd had new carpets installed, but the curtains were the ones she had chosen, the light blue walls in the living room also her choice, the furniture unchanged. They did have some good times together, she remembered. She had accepted the invitation and went in fully expecting to lead discussions toward encouraging Marco to increase sales of previous vintages, but the first thing she said was, "You've really kept up the place. I've forgotten how nice this house is."

"I've always hoped . . . Never mind," he said.

Anna pushed down the memories that floated up to her consciousness and went ahead with her reason for coming to dinner. "I've been thinking about ways we might increase sales so we can meet the monthly payments on the winery equipment."

She went on to explain plans for contacting restaurants and wine houses and especially the new wine shops that were selling gourmet meals along with tasting flights of wine. She offered to do part of the footwork herself whenever she could.

Marco smiled as she made her suggestions. He nodded agreement to most of what she was saying because he had already implemented most of those ideas, but he knew her personal contacts wouldn't hurt. She finally interrupted herself and asked, "What is that wonderful aroma coming from the oven?"

"It's a simple dish: *Peperoni Ripieni Di Riso E Salsiccia.*"

"Doesn't sound simple."

"Just stuffed peppers with rice and sausage." He handed her a bottle of her earlier Immelhoff Zinfandel to open. "We'll have grilled snow peas with toasted almonds for our vegetable, and I bought some mascarpone for dessert. Didn't have time to make that."

"You are amazing." She quickly removed the cork from the wine bottle and poured two glasses of the red full-bodied wine. "I'm glad you kept some of this Zinfandel before Dad started turning it into white Zin. I like it much better." She handed him a glass.

Marco accepted the glass, clinked it against hers and said, "Salute! This is to us."

"You mean to our success in defeating Stanton's assault on the winery?"

"No. I mean to us as a couple, a married couple. I think it's time we got realistic about our relationship. Even your archenemy half-cousin knows there's something peculiar about our affair. I think it's time we came out of hiding."

"But I don't care what other people think about how we live our lives."

"Neither am I concerned about what others think," Marco said. "It's what it's doing to us. We get together at night. We're close as any couple could be, and then during the day we live as though we are not even friends but continuous adversaries. It's a ridiculous relationship, and it's not doing either of us any good. By your own admission, you get depressed; and I'm in a constant quandary. I believe it's time we change things. Either we admit to ourselves that we are still a couple, or we go our separate ways."

Anna knew he was probably right. She had always accused him of being indecisive, but realized it was time for her to make a decision. They should either live together or break up the relationship completely. Strangely enough because he sounded so definite, she respected that in him. Her answer was not quite what he expected. "Do you mind if we have your dinner first, and then I will give you my answer?"

"No. I've waited this long. I also have something else to tell you, but not until we first settle what's going to happen between us. The information shouldn't, but somehow might, affect your decision."

"Now you have caught my attention."

"Know this," Marco said, "whatever you decide I will always care for you."

Anna squinted her eyes and looked directly at Marco. She saw something in his eyes and his manner that caused her to realize, realistically, perhaps for the first time since their breakup, that she could actually lose him and what that loss would mean to her.

Marco slipped on a pair of padded gloves and slid the baking dish with the stuffed peppers out of the oven. He served the dishes steaming hot and said nothing more that would lead her either way toward making a decision.

Anna ate, not saying much except for occasional compliments on Marco's cooking and taking sips of her own satisfying Zinfandel. Finally she said, "Well, you know I have been thinking."

Marco's heart skipped a couple of beats, but he remained patient.

"You said you were serving mascarpone for dessert. Well, we should probably have a sweet wine with your dessert, but I unfortunately don't make any of those."

"That's what you were thinking about, dessert wine?" He paused and drew in a deep breath to keep his emotions under control. "I bought a fine Malvasia from the Paso Robles region."

"You have thought of everything then, haven't you?"

"No. I haven't figured out how to bring you around to deciding on our future."

"You're absolutely certain about us, and that we would be able to live together and get along while we're at it?"

"The more you procrastinate, the less sure I am."

"Ooh!" she said. "That hurts." Still she remained quiet, tapping her lips with her fingers, before saying, "Bring out the Malvasia. Let's drink a sweet toast to the future."

Marco started after the wine, but before getting to the wine in the cooler, he realized she had said toast the future not their future. He stopped and returned to Anna. She knew what was coming so she stood up to meet him, returning an emotion-filled embrace by which she meant yes, but even then never actually said the word.

When they finally pulled apart, she asked, "What else was it you were going to tell me?"

"First we must have that sweet drink to seal our almost decision and then we have to make another important choice, one that involves both of us."

"I don't much care for secrets."

"I'm not exactly keeping a secret from you, just considering the timing."

Marco went after the wine, motioned for her to sit, opened the bottle and slowly poured two slim glasses of the clear liquid. But in taking his time, he realized he was establishing a precedent, attempting to gain partial control of their relationship, something which was sadly lacking in their earlier life together.

After a couple sips of wine and a bite of mascarpone, Marco said, "I know you liked this house when we lived here, but I notice you didn't mind moving away from it into your family home when we split up."

Anna, always a little impatient, said, "Get to the point."

"I believe I have a solution to one of your problems. I have a solid offer on this house. It's now worth three times what we paid for it, and you know half of whatever we get is yours. But if we re-establish our marriage, it can be all yours. You could solve the winery's financial problems in a hurry."

"You're going too fast for me." Anna held up both hands, palms facing Marco. "If you sell this house, where would you live?"

"No. Where would we live? Remember we are talking about getting back together. We'd have to check with Joseph first. If he agrees, we could start out by living in your family home for now."

Anastasia cradled her forehead in her hands. "Hold on, Marco. This is all coming too fast for me." She had never before known Marco to make such important judgments.

She pushed away from the table and stood. "This has been a momentous evening. I think I'd better leave now. I have to sleep with all these choices—but not with you tonight. I must consider the consequences of all that you have suggested."

"One more thing." Marco smiled. "If it works out, I think we should throw a big party, call it a coming out, a resurgence, or simply a harvest celebration. Whatever you like. But we will hold off letting friends and relatives know what we are celebrating until then, except for your father, of course. What do you think?"

"I think my internal processor is about to crash. Are you the same man I used to know?"

"Maybe this time it would be as though you are starting out with a new man: bound to cause different results."

Anna grabbed her purse and keys and practically ran out of the house.

None of her responses went unnoticed. Marco was satisfied that he had brought the relationship to a crisis, but observing her reactions, he could only shake his head at her hesitancy.

* * *

Donald Stanton had been visiting the Napa Valley far more often than either Anna or Marco had ever known. His visits were always at night, well after dark. On several occasions, he had seen Marco park his pickup truck down the street from the Immelhoff property and walk surreptitiously into the house via a back door. After Marco was safely inside, Donald would covertly survey the grounds slowly examining the equipment, the barn, the vineyards, the winery, all the while planning the route he might take to accomplish his real goal.

When he first discovered the large doors at the top of the loading ramp to the barn were swung shut but not always padlocked, he pulled one open and slid inside. There he found one of the items he was searching for. The Chardonnay cuttings Anna had taken back were stacked along one side where the horse stalls used to be. I'll take care of those later, he thought to himself.

He shuffled across the building to the big-wheeled tractor. He climbed aboard and thought about starting it, but it had been disarmed. Anyhow he realized driving that around inside the barn was probably a bad idea. It would have been too noisy and he might have been caught, but he was saddened thinking about how much terror to the equipment and building he could've done. No, I have a great idea which I'll save for a better time, he consoled himself. This one will really bring havoc to the Pugliesi clan.

Donald felt he had accomplished something on this latest exploration, at least now he had a plan which would help devastate these reluctant relatives, and he figured he could easily pull it off without exposure. He quietly closed the big door, walked off the grounds and down the highway to where he had parked his long, black sedan.

* * *

In the morning, a gnarly old pickup truck carrying a dozen newly made barrels followed by a large stake-bed truck carrying several dozen more barrels rolled up the driveway and stopped outside the *Immelhoff Winery*. Stavos, the cooper, stepped out of the old pickup. The driver and a tall young man exited the larger truck. Joseph saw them arrive and went out to greet the men.

Stavos extended his hand. "I suppose you know about these barrels, Joseph. Your daughter ordered them a few weeks ago."

"Yes, she informed me. I'm sure she'll be very happy to see them when she returns from town. Let's roll these inside to the third tunnel in the winery. We can surprise her when she gets back."

"Joseph, have you met my son, Steven Stavos?"

"No, and a handsome young man he is, too." Joseph shook hands with Steve. The driver of the large truck was not introduced but as soon as he stepped out of his truck, he informed everyone in a nasty, disgruntled tone he had to leave as soon as they unloaded his truck.

They all got to work immediately unloading the big rig first. When they had set the last barrel on the ground, the morose driver climbed into his vehicle and drove off without saying a word to anyone.

"Last time I'll ever use that grouch," Stavos said.

"You're lucky," Steve explained to his father. "I heard him bellyache all the way over. He wasn't getting paid enough, his back hurt, gasoline cost too much, his wife spends money before he even sees it, his house roof leaks, his truck tires are bald. I thought we'd never get here."

"Son, I appreciate your riding with him. Since he was prepaid for the delivery, I didn't trust him at all. I was afraid he might disappear with our cooperage."

"I know, Dad. It was like riding shotgun, only having to hold the shotgun on the driver."

The three of them unloaded the pickup and then began the task of rolling the barrels into the winery.

Before they finished, Anna pulled up the drive in her Cherokee. Seeing the barrels, she ran up to Stavos and greeted him with a big hug. "Talk about arriving right on time. You are wonderful."

She examined one of the barrels. The first thing she noticed pleased her very much. "You treated the outside of the barrels against mildew, just what we would have done."

"After they dried out," Stavos explained. "If you look inside, you'll see that we also let them soak with water for a while to be sure they didn't leak."

"First class! We can use them right away to start aging the Emma Mae Cabernet. Hold on. I have your check for the balance of payment." She started to run inside, but stopped and turned to face Stavos. "We're hosting a party here soon. Would you like to come? You are invited. Bring your wife and this handsome young man. Who is he, by the way?"

"My son, Steven Stavos."

"Well, there'll be some pretty girls he might be interested in."

"What? No one for me?" Stavos asked.

"Get to work, Pop, before you're in trouble," Steve quipped while he rolled a barrel purposely close barely missing his father's foot. Steve had returned recently from attending his second year of college in Athens, Greece. The experience living in a foreign country was good for him, but he was happy to be home so he could get involved in local sports, see his friends and to be able to speak to people without consulting a dictionary.

On his next trip out for another barrel, after Anna came out with the check for Stavos, Joseph said to her, "What was that about a party?"

"Yes. I was so excited about the new barrels arriving that I just let it out."

"Nothing wrong with being spontaneous. What's the occasion?"

"Do we need a reason for a party? The harvest is in, the wine is doing well, most of it anyhow. We just want to celebrate."

"There's something you're not telling me, isn't there?" Joseph asked. "Who is this *we* you're talking about?"

"I'll explain after we finish getting the rest of these barrels inside. Before we discuss a party, we have some work to do. I think you mentioned to Freddie that the Emma Mae was ready to go to the press. Well, this time I agree with you. We can also transfer it right into the new barrels. Let's start first thing in the morning."

* * *

Early the next morning Oscar and two of his cousins came in to help. Using gravity for power, one of the men controlled the flow of must down to the basket press. Federica handled the controls for the large press. The other man gathered the pomace and carried it out to the compost pile. Anna fed the juice into the barrels with Oscar rolling the filled ones out and the fresh ones in. While Federica was being careful to use light pressure, she stayed close to the fermented wine. At first she savored the aroma, but then began swaying from the effect of the fumes, as though she had too much to drink.

Anna saw what was happening to her sister. She turned off the electric power to the press. "Go outside, Freddie, you're getting drunk."

"I . . . guess, I . . . guess, maybe I better get some air."

One of the men kept her from falling as she staggered outside.

Anna took control of the press making sure she didn't inhale too much of the sweet intoxicating fumes.

After all of the wine had been stored in the barrels and stacked in one of the tunnels for aging, Anna finally relaxed in their living room. Her father was reading a wine review about the success of recent wineries in Chile and South Africa when Anna interrupted his concentration.

"Dad, would you mind putting that magazine down for a minute?"

"Of course not. What is it?" He stopped reading the article and gave her his attention, actually pleased with the kindness he detected in her manner.

"I've been thinking: You know *Immelhoff Winery* is not much of an appellation. It is so outdated. It sounds like last century. I told Federica that it has no romance, no allure. She didn't say much, but I believe she agreed. I'd like to change our name. Well, I've finally decided on a name I want. I'd like to call this winery the *Dancing Horse Winery*. What do you think?"

"Do you really want to know what I think?"

"About this, yes. I'd like to announce the name at the party I mentioned, if we have one. If that's all right with you? I know it's a big move, but I think it would give us a new outlook."

"A new name would be fine with me. I won't fight you on it, but you know there already is an Iron Horse Winery, and a Crazy Horse Winery."

"So you don't like it?"

"I didn't say that at all. Actually I like the sound of it. I never would have thought of making a name change like that," Joseph admitted. "Also I want to say I've never you seen you quite this way before. Whatever the change is I like it."

"There is one more thing. I hope you don't make too much out of what I'm going to say now." She paused for a few moments to prepare herself. "Marco and I might be getting back together. We're wondering if it works out, could we live here with you for a while? He wants to sell our house so we can help with the financial problems here at *Dancing Horse*."

Joseph did not answer right away. Finally he said, "Wonderful!"

"You mean about selling the house?"

"No, I mean about all of it. I approve wholeheartedly, especially about you getting back with Marco. Come here." He pulled his daughter close to him and kissed her on both cheeks.

She returned the affection, but then said, "Now, don't make this out to be a big deal. Actually so far, I haven't given him my answer. I'm just testing the water. You know you can never be sure how things might work out."

"You can be certain about Marco. You've known him long enough to know he's a fine young man and a good partner."

"Okay, that's enough. Now I have to get busy moving the Chardonnay to the redwood cask. I want to fine it with bentonite and let it settle for awhile and then remove the lees. If that's all right with you. I know you usually handle the Chardonnay yourself."

"It's what I wanted to do anyhow; so, yes, you can go ahead. Do you mean to start right now, tonight?"

"No, of course not, but first thing in the morning."

"Okay. I was wondering, is Marco coming to visit you again tonight?"

"No. He's in Atlanta. Wait a minute! Are you talking about him seeing me during the night? Are you telling me you have known about these visits all along?"

"Well, I may've been born in the last century, but I don't live in it."

Anna felt the sting, but she still had more to tell her father. "I don't know how to approach this next matter. But since we're being so frank with each other, I guess I'll just come out with it."

"Sounds serious."

"Yes. It's a matter of business, winemaking business. I'm sure you heard about how I fooled around with the yeast and nearly ruined the latest harvest of Cabernet."

"It hasn't been a secret around here, though you never discussed it with me. As I remember, you said you were using an old-world technique."

Anna felt the rebuke and didn't respond because she knew she deserved it. "I've been sampling it for the last two days. Well, it's not bad; however, I don't like the way it's going. I had thought I might be able to make a Cabernet Rosé out of it. Now I've also changed my mind about that. I wouldn't want an inferior wine to go out under our label, especially our new label."

"Where does that leave us?"

"Well, these days there are a lot of bulk wines on the market, many of them not nearly as good as this concoction of mine. Do you know any of those entrepreneurs the French call *negociants* who turn bulk wine into a marketable brand?"

"No, but Marco probably would."

"I had hoped not to bring him into this."

"Why not? Right now he handles all of our sales."

"If I talk with him, he'll want to know what I have decided about our relationship, and I'm not quite ready to settle that."

CHAPTER 11

The wooden-framed trellis, built out from the highway-facing side of the stone winery, interlaced with old vine growth, made a perfect cover for a long dinner table which was itself strewn with flowers and overflowing tureens of translucent white and deep purple grapes.

Oscar's wife, Maya, a sociable, attractive, energetic woman, with help from Federica and the slim, sweet-mannered Leticia, were all placing silverware and glasses next to a variety of plates necessary for the coming meal.

When Stavos turned off the highway to enter the Pugliesi property, he saw the women working around the table, but brought his old character of a pickup truck to an immediate stop.

"What's wrong?" his son Steve asked.

"Look up there. Where is the *Immelhoff Winery* sign? Are you sure we're in the right place?"

"Of course."

"You remember the hand-carved wooden sign? I remember since I was a boy seeing it every time we passed this way. Do you think maybe the surprise is the Pugliesis are throwing a party because the winery is up for sale?"

"I doubt that, Dad. Let's go ahead and find out."

As they drove up the drive, Stavos pointed out the buildings which he knew on sight, but still wasn't sure they weren't intruding on a stranger's land.

"It's all right," he finally said. "I recognize Mrs. Mendez, the vineyard manager's wife, and Federica, Anna's sister. Who is that pretty girl with them?"

"I hope to find out," Steve said.

"Be careful, son. She might be the very one they brought for me. You don't want to ruin the party before it starts."

Steve chuckled, but he wasn't quite sure if his father was joking or not.

Federica carried out the introductions all around. "Mr. Stavos, where is your wife?"

"My wife? Oh, she's not here. She has what you call hypochon . . . something. She is always sick."

Steven normally defended his mother, but he had suddenly become occupied with someone else.

Federica smiled when she noticed Steve holding Leticia's hand a few moments longer than customary after an introduction. She then spoke to both Steve and his father: "I'm glad you men are here. Marco hasn't shown up yet, and my father is on an errand in town. We need your strong arms to carry out the food and drinks, but first, would you guys go over to the barn and bring out the folding chairs? We stacked them just inside the door."

Stavos nodded and headed for the barn.

Steve wanted to talk with Leticia, but he thought he might save that for later. He went along with his father to gather the folding chairs.

About then Joseph returned with a large order of antipasti he had arranged from a take-out deli in Rutherford. Federica and Leticia helped him carry the packages to the long table. The women placed the roasted shrimp, fresh greens, sauces, and a variety of bread and cheeses along the center in an attractive arrangement.

Joseph walked over to greet his former wife's parents who had just arrived from Sonoma. They were an older couple, a bit shaky, but still able to drive and enjoy their retirement. They never missed a chance to be with their granddaughters and especially their great grandson, Sandy.

Scott with his son Sandy arrived soon after. Sandy aimed his new camera like a weapon taking shots at anyone and anything that interested him.

They were followed by two more vehicles with several of Anna's friends from San Francisco. The first was a steel-gray Porsche Carrera driven by a handsome young fellow whose wild, dark curly hair shifted with the quick jerks of his head as it moved from side to side like a bobble-headed doll while he was shaking hands with everyone. He was proud to show off his new car and newer girlfriend, Cindy, who was quite pretty but much quieter than anyone would have expected to be accompanying Chip Calahan, a swinging corporate lawyer who worked for the San Francisco 49ers.

The second car with Abbey, Anna's closest friend and college roommate, and her husband Dale, a smooth talker who did some kind of work with a computer games company, though no one was quite sure what.

Anna greeted her friends, got them seated and then poured a Pinot Noir to get things started. Steve made certain he sat beside Leticia whose smile didn't discourage him, but then she also smiled at his father so he wasn't at all sure about her.

When Sandy saw the Porsche arrive, he stopped taking pictures of people and concentrated on the car, using both his zoom and close-up lens which he deftly aimed and quickly composed each shot.

Marco had still not appeared, so Anna went inside the house to make a phone call. She had called him several times during the day with no luck. It was by then late Saturday afternoon, so on a chance she tried his office. Marco's secretary informed her that Marco had left earlier about noontime for the San Francisco airport to catch a flight to Fort Lauderdale, Florida.

"Did he leave me a message?" Anna asked.

"Yes. He said if you called to tell you he'd get in touch with you."

"That's it?"

"Is there a problem?"

"No. Everything is just fine!" She slammed the phone down and sat long enough to gather her thoughts. Since the dinner Marco had served her in their house, he had not returned for his nightly visits. Of course, that was her idea. Since that dinner, their contacts had all been by phone. Only then did she realize how much she missed those intimate visits. When he asked if she had made a decision about the two of them, she still resisted answering the question. Instead she spoke with him about the invitations and the date she had set for the party he had suggested, informing everyone there would be a surprise announcement, but would not let Marco know what that might be.

Maya Mendez came in the house to inquire about the entrée of well-seasoned Mexican dishes she had prepared.

"Yes, I think it's ready," Anna said, as cheerily as she could. "Let's rescue the menudo and fajitas with the bell peppers from the stove and feed our guests."

The meal went well. Joseph brought out some of their estate Cabernet which he served to everyone except Sandy and Leticia who got all the soft drinks they wanted.

Anna knew she eventually would have to get up and say something about why the party had been called. She was completely puzzled about why Marco would go on a business trip at this inopportune time. While she was mulling that over, a motorcyclist roared up the driveway and slid to a stop.

"Telegram for . . ." He paused when he looked at the name. "Anastasia Pugliesi." He tried reading it aloud but mangled every syllable.

Anna stepped forward to accept the message. "I didn't know people still sent telegrams."

"Of course they do, ma'am. Don't take away my livelihood." He waited expectantly, so she gave him a five-dollar tip. With that he spun his vehicle around and roared off. Anna opened the telegram. It was from Marco:

> FOUND THREE RESTAURANTS TO FEATURE CABERNET –(STOP)– SORRY ABOUT MISSING PARTY –(STOP)– REALIZE NO ANSWER IS ANSWER ENOUGH –(STOP)– BEST WISHES FOR FUTURE –(STOP)– MARCO

She almost crumpled the note, controlled herself, then folded it neatly and returned to the arbor and her guests.

Even after the food had been devoured, plenty of wine consumed, a tray of cheese and fruit passed around and then a generous cut of tiramisu served to each guest, she didn't try to explain what the surprise was she had mentioned with her invitation. Marco's telegram had pulled off a surprise enough of its own.

Anna's friends noted her unusually quiet manner so they had engaged in conversations with Oscar and Maya Mendez whose friendly manner made them feel at home. The sun had set behind the Mayacamas, yet no one except Joseph's elder in-laws had thought about leaving. Leticia was balancing her time talking with Steve and Stavos, not flirting, just being her pleasant self. She liked Steve but figured at twenty he was a bit too old for her, and she really enjoyed talking to his father because he had some great real and imagined stories to tell.

Anna went around visiting but was really avoiding making any announcements. Marco's letter put her in a state of bewilderment. She admitted to herself he was right about a no-answer being an answer. Now she had to say something about a surprise, but was not sure hearing about a name change for the winery would be enough.

Stavos was the one who finally saved Anna. "Anna," he said when she strolled by, "when we drove in, my boy and me, I didn't see the *Immelhoff Winery* sign up at the entrance. Does that mean you are selling the winery?"

A groan came from several voices.

"No, Stavos, my good friend. That has to do with the surprise I had promised everyone. I"—she looked to her father—"we . . . have decided to change the name to *Dancing Horse Winery.* We want to update our name while we upgrade our wine. What do you think?"

Stavos raised his glass. "Change can be good. Let's drink to your success!" He clinked his glass with Anna's.

Oscar Mendez then tapped a fork against his glass to gain attention even though his wife was trying to get him not to say anything. "All I want to say is when you break bread and drink wine with friends, you keep close to the earth. That is the best way to live." He leaned over and said to Maya, "That wasn't so bad, was it?" Maya breathed a sigh of relief, clinked her glass against his and took a hearty drink.

Steve was constantly glancing at the young beautiful Leticia who was then sitting across the table. Her eyes were light brown, enhanced by long dark lashes. She had the most amiable easygoing manner, also quite self-composed. Steve moved around so he could sit next to her.

She smiled and didn't seem troubled by his move, so he said quietly, "I wonder if we could get together sometime. You know, we could just have a coke some place in town or maybe go to a movie."

"I don't know. I mean, I like you but I'm only in high school and you're a college student; you've been to Greece and everything." Her smile just about melted him.

"I know, but I'm not going to stay in college. Now wait, that didn't come out right. I am twenty. I guess if you're sixteen that might seem like old right now, but . . ."

Steve didn't know how to continue so Leticia helped him out. "If you don't stay in college, what will you do?"

"Right now, my father has a lot of orders to fill. I've been helping him with cooperage since I returned. You know, I've been around this wine business all my life, and I kind of like it. Even in Greece, I visited wineries and vineyards. They make different wines from what we have here, a Retsina and a Mavrodaphne. Interesting tastes all right though I didn't much care for them. Dad likes them a lot. I guess it takes time for someone to learn how to appreciate the exotics."

"Do you want to become a winemaker? With your background, you'd be a natural."

"No, I'm not patient enough to become a winemaker. You have to wait years to find out if you're successful. There are other kinds of work connected to the profession. Maybe I'll ask Anna to give me a job so I can learn about other phases of the work."

"You sound ambitious, but not too sure of yourself."

"I'll get there. In the meantime, could I see you once in a while, just like a casual date?"

"I guess that would be all right."

Anna said to her friends and loud enough for everybody in general to hear, "It's getting cold out here. Why don't we go inside? I'll make some coffee, and we can all visit as long as we like."

Only the quiet elderly couple expressed their desire to leave. Joseph and Sandy walked them to their car. They hugged Joseph whom they had always treated as a son, and showered affection on Sandy. The man slipped a twenty-dollar bill in the boy's pocket. "Don't tell your Grandma," he cautioned, "or I'll be in big trouble."

After they drove off, Sandy asked his father if he could stay outside for a while to take some pictures.

"It's getting dark," Scott said.

"I know. I want to take some night shots. There's a built-in flash bulb in my camera, you know."

"Okay, but don't wander off too far."

"How far could I go? I don't have my bike with me."

As soon as Scott left him alone, Sandy didn't hesitate walking off toward the highway.

Inside the house, Chip, the lawyer, walked away from his pretty date to speak with Anna. "Hey, where's Marco? I thought for sure he would be here."

"So did I," she answered without explanation. "How do you like your coffee?"

"Straight, strong, and undiluted, like my women."

She started to ask how a woman could be undiluted, but handed him the coffee pot to pour for himself. "Later on, Chip, I'd like to speak with you about registering our new name with the county and feds or whatever is necessary. Will you advise me?"

"Certainly. I assume the winery already has state and federal permits and is registered with the Bureau of Alcohol, Tobacco, and Firearms, right?"

"Of course."

"Good! Then you should start with an online database search to be certain there are no conflicts with other wineries or companies that might be using the same name. After that I'll register it for you with the U.S. Patent and Trademark Office. Oh, and you probably would want to design a new label to go with your new outlook."

"Wow!" Anna said. "You are thorough. No wonder you've moved up so fast."

"Not as fast as I'd like."

"Now, Chip, you're doing fine. I hope I can do as well with my endeavors."

"As I see it, you're already far beyond me. Look at this remarkable operation you run. I am just one spoke in a fast-turning wheel. You are the hub that everything revolves around."

"Never mind that flattery. I'll do the research and then see about having a label designed. I'll call you soon. Right now I wouldn't want to deprive you of any more time with your date."

"Pretty on the outside, isn't she?" A cringing frown from Chip said more than his words about his real assessment of the girl he was with.

Anna's best friend approached them. "Chip, may I borrow Anna for a while?" Then to Anna, she said, "We don't see enough of you, Anna. It's been months since we've gotten together."

"I know, Abbey. The winery takes up most of my time."

"Will you try to see us more in the future?"

"I'll try, but I can't promise. There are some serious problems I still have to solve."

Federica had been walking around looking for her son. She asked Scott, "Have you seen Sandy? He seems to have disappeared."

"I let him stay outside to shoot a few pictures."

"Would you mind going out to keep an eye on him?"

Scott almost protested, but then realized his wife was right for being cautious. "Okay, honey. I'm sure he's all right."

When Scott got outside, he saw Sandy running from the vicinity of the barn toward the house yelling, "Fire! Fire!"

One side of the barn suddenly flashed into a wall of red flame. At the same time, Scott also caught sight of a man running away from the barn toward the highway.

"Dad, someone lit that fire! I saw him come out of the barn. When he saw me, he took off running."

"Could you describe him?"

"He was all in black, even had on a black hood."

"Did you take a picture of him?"

"No. It happened so fast."

By that time people were coming out from the house. Oscar Mendez and Joseph were leading the group. By the time they reached the barn, the flames had reached the roof shingles and had spread around two sides. Oscar quickly attached a hose to an outside faucet and started spraying water, but that stream was lost in the blaze.

Anna had stayed inside long enough to call the county fire department. Fire Chief Haggard and three firefighters arrived in less than ten minutes, but by then the barn was totally engulfed.

The dried wood in the old structure flared up so quickly very little could be done in time to save anything. Sandy finally trained his new digital camera and caught some dramatic shots of the orange-red flames overwhelming the entire building. Everything inside was lost, including the new tractor, trailers, gondolas, an old stake-bed truck, the pruning knives, serpettes, heating pots, miscellaneous equipment, and all the Chardonnay cuttings from the Carneros property which Anna had been saving to plant on the upper soil near the foothills.

The fire captain noticed Sandy taking the pictures so he asked him, as had his father, whether he had shot any of the man they saw running away.

"No. I'm sorry. It happened so fast I didn't think about that."

"What were you shooting before?" he asked the boy.

"I was trying to take some pictures of cool cars," he said. "The only really cool one was the gray Porsche sitting in the driveway, but then I spotted a black BMW parked down the road a ways. I walked over there and shot that one, too."

"May I see your camera?"

"Sure."

The captain checked the LCD monitor on the camera, scrolling until he came to the cars Sandy mentioned. He had taken several pictures of both cars from various angles.

"Does this BMW belong to any one here?" he asked the group clustered around him.

"No," Anna said, "but I know someone who owns one exactly like that."

"Let's go have a look and see if it's still there."

They walked out to the highway. Sandy showed him where the car had been parked, but, of course, it was gone.

"Do you mind if I borrow the memory card from your camera, young man? We can print these out and probably get the license plate number."

"Not necessary," Anna said. "I know whose car it is. It belongs to Donald Stanton."

"How do you know that?"

"I'd bet the barn on it."

"If you're right you'd win the bet, but unfortunately you've lost the barn."

"Not very funny," she said. "I've already reported another incident to the police. I'm certain this is from the same person who tampered with our fermentation tanks."

"I'd like to hear more about the individual."

Anna was more than willing to tell the whole story to the captain, which she did.

After she finished, he had to ask, "Why are you so certain this 'person of interest' is the same individual who perpetrated these events?"

"Because he is supposedly a half-cousin with the demented notion that he should have inherited our property."

"Should he have?"

"Absolutely not! What are you implying?"

"He has motivation."

"Does that justify attempting to destroy our wine and burning our barn?"

"Of course not." The captain held off saying anything else until Anna settled down, and then he added, "We'll investigate the fire tonight, and I'll speak with the sheriff's office first thing tomorrow."

Anna's party guests had followed most of this conversation. They expressed their sympathy and support and began leaving, except for Chip who was following everything closely.

He approached Anna. "I don't do criminal law, but if I can help you, let me know."

"I will, Chip. I feel better just having you here."

He gave her a nice hug and kissed her lightly on the cheek, before leading his pretty but not too exciting date to his new Porsche.

* * *

About midmorning Fire Chief Haggard called her office to inform Anna what he had learned from the photos and the burn search that had been performed. "Gasoline started the fire. We also did an enlargement of the boy's photos which produced a clear picture of a license plate. It's registered to a Donald Stanton."

"Yes! He's the one I was telling you about. Are you going to arrest him?"

"Hold on for a minute. I have turned all this info over to the county sheriff; however, I must warn you what we have is only circumstantial evidence. No one identified the man who was seen running from the barn."

"But you know for sure Stanton's car was parked out there, and you said he had motive."

"All very true. We'll let the Calistoga Police Department do their work now. They are very competent people."

Reluctantly she thanked him, hung up the phone and thought to herself, I'm not so sure about that.

She phoned Chip and couldn't reach him, but just then Marco came strolling into the winery. Anna saw him through the office window in animated conversation with her father. Instead of coming over to see her, he walked with Joseph out to inspect the remains of the old barn. When they returned, they came directly into her office.

Anna addressed Marco with controlled anger. "You have a lot of nerve coming here after what you did."

"I didn't do anything," Marco defended himself, a relaxed smile on his face.

"I mean, what you didn't do. Don't confuse me. I'm upset enough after what happened last night."

"Because of the fire, I don't blame you."

"And the way you let me down."

"If I let you down, it was because of choices you did not make, not because of anything I did."

"I was planning to make an announcement which would prove I had made a decision."

"Which was?"

"Too late now. You ran off as though you didn't care to know my choice."

"Fate is the vengeance of choices unmade."

"You're terrible," she said. "Don't start quoting Greek philosophy to me."

"Since getting mixed up with you again, philosophy is about all I have to hold on to."

"Then I hope you're satisfied," she said.

"Not at all, but I found waiting for you is waiting in vain. Why should I continue?"

Joseph couldn't stand by any more; he had to speak up. "If you two could just stop and listen to yourselves, you would be disgusted with your bantering. If you try talking with each other, you might be able to find common ground."

Marco shook his head. "Maybe it is too late."

"You might have called me and explained that you had to be away. You left me giving a party for us and sent a telegram from a safe distance. Is that any way to get back together?"

"No," Marco said. "It's not, but I'm not apologizing. You should have given me an answer before the party. I have often enough made my feelings clear to you. Why should I be left dangling like a puppet? I'm not pleading with you any more. I have decided to move on."

"That suits me fine. Dad, will you please fire this man right now?"

"Why would I fire Marco?"

"He should not be a part of this winery."

"Because you can't get along doesn't change how effective Marco is for our winery. Besides, I enjoy working with him."

"I don't want to work with anyone as obstinate as he is, and someone who obviously will let us down the way he does."

"I don't believe Marco is obstinate. I've always found him to be a thoughtful, cooperative person. I understand you may feel hurt, but he didn't let us down. He made new contacts while he was away."

"Now the two of you are joining forces against me."

Marco had lost the calm demeanor he came in with. "I've heard that argument from you before. Perhaps you should examine yourself, Anna. The problem is not always with someone else."

"This is my office! I want the two of you to get out of here."

Marco smiled in a way that Anna couldn't understand. He nodded his head and walked out. Joseph gestured with both hands out, palms up, shrugged and left her alone in the office.

He caught up with Marco before he got out of the building. "Wait up, Marco."

Marco stopped by the large doors and waited patiently for Joseph to explain.

"I have to talk with you, but it's not about Anna. I'll certainly let you two work that out in your own way."

"Thank you. I appreciate your support in there."

"I meant what we were talking about earlier," Joseph said. "Besides losing the barn, and having the winery under siege from an unstable person, we have about two thousand gallons of recently fermented wine that we don't want to sell under our label. I was hoping you might have contacts who are actively seeking to purchase volumes of nouveau wine. It's not aged as yet, but it is salvageable. Anna finally told me what happened. I have tested it and have to agree with her about this batch. It's certainly not up to our standards."

"Is that the wine that she experimented with using an unproven yeast?"

"Yes, but I don't blame her for what happened. Winemakers have to experiment in order to improve their product."

"Maybe you should blame her. She, and no one else, is responsible."

"I've never heard you quite this adamant before, Marco. You're sounding like a different person."

"I've been doing a lot of thinking, Mr. Pugliesi. I still love your daughter, but life with her is impossible. So as I said, I'm ready to move on."

"That will remain between the two of you. I'm out of the loop you two are swinging around each other. But will you help me, us, with moving the wine? I figure we might find someone who would buy it in bulk perhaps to be blended with other similar stock."

"Of course. There's a lot of that two-dollar starter stuff on the market and those willing to make more. I'm sure I can move yours."

"Great," Joseph said. "If you don't mind, I'm going to call Anna out here. I think she'll be pleased about this."

"That would be a welcome change."

Joseph went into the winery and explained what Marco had just promised. She actually came out to thank Marco for his offer.

Unexpectedly Steven Stavos drove in. He waited in his pickup until the two had finished talking and walked up to Anna, but before he had a chance to say anything, she explained to him, "Leticia is not here. She's in school."

"I know," Steve said. "I wanted a chance to talk with you. Hello, Mr. Preziano, we missed you at the party."

"Call me Marco."

"Yes, sir. Now that you're here I'd like to ask both of you the same question. I've been working on the periphery of the wine business with my father. I don't especially want to make wine, but I would like to discover what other kinds of work there might be in the wine world."

"Are you good with mechanical things?" Anna asked.

"Well, yes, I not only work with the cooperage, but I'm trying to develop one of those machines that build barrels as good as the hand-crafted ones. One barrel at a time is much too slow for me."

"Interesting. I could use an energetic hand here. I always have to call my brother-in-law when the machinery goes berserk."

Marco said, "I can see a lot of potential for you in other ways. You're courteous; you speak well. There's always a salesperson or an entrepreneur who comes along with ideas to shake things up. You might be one of those. I could take you on as assistant."

"Hold on," Anna cut in. "He came here to see me. I can always use intelligent energetic help. But I have one more question for you, Steve. What would your father say about this?"

"Oh, he is an old-world craftsman, only he is about to retire. He would rather have me stay on and become a cooper."

"What is wrong with that?"

"Nothing really, except that heating and bending barrel staves for eternity is not for me. He is so proud of his work, and I am very proud of him. He is a craftsman artist, but individual craftsmen like my father are becoming obsolete."

"I certainly hope not. I'm attempting to craft wine as good or better than those from the old world."

"That's why I'd like to work for you. You appreciate the past but you are moving into the future. I want to be a part of that."

"You're hired!" She waited for a reaction from Marco, but he remained stoic. She indirectly spoke to Marco by addressing Steve, "Maybe on occasion, if Marco treats me right, I'll let you work with him for a while. I'm confident you will learn a lot. Though he doesn't know it, he already is an accomplished entrepreneur himself."

Marco heard the compliment. Coming from Anna, it almost took his breath away. He kept his wits about him, nodded, and said quietly, "Thank you, Anna. I'll go make a few calls now to find out who might be able to use some bulk wine." He drove off wondering if Anna could really be coming around to him. Well, he thought, sometimes hope is just around the corner. But no, he knew better than to let that thought linger: a compliment is not a commitment, especially not from her.

Anna had already moved on to her next task. She said to Steve who was on the verge of leaving, "Would you be able to start Saturday morning?"

"Yes. I'll check with my father, of course, but I think we can work it out."

"Good. Freddie will be moving our Chardonnay from the stainless steel down to a redwood vat. You'll have a chance to learn a little about processing white wine and also something about two technologies: modern stainless steel tanks, and antiquated redwood casks. I don't suppose your father ever made those."

"Not that I've ever heard. What does the redwood do for the wine?"

"Nothing. It's not like oak. Redwood doesn't influence the taste at all. We just use it for storage. One other thing you might like to know; Leticia is scheduled to be here Saturday."

"Oh, that's nice to hear. Thank you. In that case, I'll be certain to be here."

CHAPTER 12

After all the negative things that had happened to Anna, the good interaction she had with Steven Stavos raised her mood enough to enable her to believe that good things could happen again. She felt sure the sun would rise for her again the next day. It did with clear crisp skies and a distinctive fall chill in the air. She pulled on a sweatshirt over her usual work clothing and went outside to examine the aftermath of the celebration. The burnt mass of the classic old barn presented a difficult scene for her to acknowledge. She hadn't been able to approach the devastation the day before because the fire chief wanted everything left as it was so his people could search through it for evidence. He said she could begin clearing the debris the next day; however, she was reluctant to walk through the remains of the once red classic barn.

What Anna didn't know was that Oscar had brought his wife along to help with cleaning up from the party. She saw that Federica was already at work along with Maya removing the party debris from under and around the arbor. She asked Oscar and Joseph, who was already outside with the others, if they would start clearing out the rubble from the burn. They quickly got on that job, hurling the heavier chunks of charred wood and ruined pieces of equipment into the back of Oscar's pickup truck and raking through the burn, rescuing the items which could be saved.

Anna somberly joined the women by tossing empty bottles, paper plates, and cartons into the trash. Maya gathered the wineglasses and silverware which she carried inside to be washed.

Working with the others, Anna began to feel better. She addressed Federica, "Good thing we're not in the growing season. It's getting colder every night. I believe it's time we cleaned out the rest of Dad's old barrels in case he wants to use them for his purposes. I want to keep my hands off them in case I get tempted to do something crazy again. What do you think, Freddie?"

"I think you're slowly getting your senses back," Federica said, knowing Anna's none-too-subtle remark was meant for her to get started as soon as possible. "I'll get to that as soon as Maya and I finish what we're doing here."

Anna walked toward the winery, her mind never really leaving the concern she had for operating the winery, but also carrying an extra burden of anger she felt toward her would-be cousin. Before she entered her office, she heard the phone ringing, pulling her out of the clamor of unsettling thoughts bouncing around in her head.

"Yes. Who is it?" she asked with a bite to her words.

"Detective Schmidt. I've been assigned to investigate your complaints."

"Do you call burning down our barn a complaint?"

He didn't respond to her sarcasm but continued with a practiced monotone, matter-of-fact tone, "Fire Chief Haggard presented us with photos of a car taken by an eleven-year-old boy. He also told us that a man no one could identify was seen walking toward the highway.

"I read the report you filed earlier about some mysterious person who supposedly changed the temperature gauges on your fermentation tanks. No fingerprints or evidence was found to substantiate that claim."

"Well, you have a license number which proves who owns the car that was parked nearby just before the fire started. His name is Donald Stanton. I'm sure you know that already. Aren't you going to question him?"

"A car was parked along the highway. Nothing illegal about that. We don't have much to go on. Tell me, do you have insurance on the barn and the wine stored in those tanks?"

"There's insurance on the barn, and insurance on our property. I guess you could call aging wine our property. Anyway, what are you insinuating? I wouldn't sabotage my own winery!"

"It's been known to happen."

"This is a very frustrating conversation. Are you going to question Donald Stanton or not?"

"There has to be more to go on. We can't pull a man in for questioning with what little you've given us."

"His car was parked near our property and gone immediately after the fire started. What more do you need?"

"I understand a party was going on. Wine was being served. Maybe you're not too clear on the details. Perhaps this Stanton was a guest."

"He was no guest here."

"I don't know that."

"The hell you don't! I just *told* you!"

"No need to raise your voice. My investigation will require that I speak with the man in question. If there are any other developments, I'll inform you. That'll be all for now." He hung up the phone.

Anna expelled a blast of air in frustration.

* * *

Detective Schmidt did more than just talk with Stanton on the phone. He phoned him to arrange a face-to-face interview, then later drove to San Francisco so he could observe Donald's reaction while under questioning.

"What do you know about the *Dancing Horse Winery's* barn-burning incident?"

"I don't even know there is such a winery. I've never heard of it."

"Your car was photographed parked close to the property."

"Are you talking in riddles? If you are, I don't have time for this nonsense."

Schmidt placed his glasses on his long, slim nose and glanced down at his notes before proceeding. "You'll have to take the time, Mr. Stanton, or you might end up serving time."

"You think you're being clever?" Donald turned away from the detective and then stared back at him. "This is certainly no way to conduct an interview."

Schmidt flipped one page back in his notebook, realizing he had scratched out *Immelhoff Winery* and written in *Dancing Horse Winery*, but he continued without apologizing for his error, just asked another question: "Did you not know that the *Immelhoff Winery* has been renamed the *Dancing Horse Winery*?"

"No. That's news to me."

"Same question still applies: why was your car parked near the property?"

"I was passing by, saw lights and music, stopped to see what was going on."

"Were you invited to the affair?"

"No, but there's something you don't understand here. I'm related to that family. Mr. Pugliesi is my uncle, so I should have been invited."

"That's not much of a defense. What do you know about changing temperature gauges on fermentation tanks?"

"Not much. I'm no winemaker. How long is this going to take? I have work to do."

"Just keep calm, sir. Not much longer. I notice you get more irritated as we speak. Your foot tapping is a sure giveaway, a clear indication you are hiding something. You haven't been very cooperative, but I'm willing to give you a little more time. Is there anything you'd care to volunteer regarding your case which might enlighten me?"

"No. I don't know what it is you think I would have to say."

"We can't ignore the evidence that you are connected to the events by your presence and your admitted relationship to the proprietors. I'll present what I have learned to the district attorney. It will be her job to decide whether to indict you or call you in for further questioning. Perhaps under oath, you will discover more than you have given me."

Schmidt folded his notebook, slipped it into a jacket pocket, shook his head thoughtfully and left.

Donald looked around the room, especially noting the other two desks separated from his by a glass wall and wondered if any of his colleagues had overheard this conversation. Everyone seemed busy with their own concerns, so he tried to return his thoughts to the numbers he was manipulating for a loan request. All he could think of was that if word of his involvement got out, and he was afraid it would, his place in the bank would be under serious scrutiny.

When he drove out of the underground parking that afternoon heading to his apartment off Union Street, he had a sinking feeling he was about to lose everything. Donald had to admit to himself that he somewhat enjoyed working for the bank. If he lost this position, he didn't have much else he cared about. The few young women he had met quickly shied away from him. He was not close to anyone on the staff he worked with, never joined in their T.G.I.F. afternoons at a local bar or even had coffee with them at lunch: all because his overriding reason for coming to San Francisco was to get control of a winery he convinced himself should have been his.

He didn't go directly to his apartment. Instead he drove through the Marina District and pulled over near the Bay where he could look out across the water. Two long, slim sculls were racing a couple of hundred yards offshore, four crew members in each craft working a pair of oars dipping and pulling in unison. Several fishing boats were slowly returning to their slips. In the distance, the graceful arches of the Golden Gate Bridge seemed to be lifting the structure up from the incoming fog.

Donald's mind stopped taking in the view as he pondered his circumstances: It's time to take a closer look at yourself. You've been obsessed. Face it. Even if you could obtain the winery, you don't know the first thing about operating one. You wouldn't give a business loan to someone who had no knowledge of what he or she was getting into. Why would you be any different if you somehow managed to gain control? You perform clandestine activities which have no honor, not an ounce of dignity in any of your covert moves. But you should realize, you have had more success than you deserve in banking. You have a good piece of property in Carneros that could be worth some money. In fact, you've done quite well considering you have not dedicated more than a fraction of your effort to your profession. Why not give banking a chance? he asked himself. Why throw it all away?

But doubts persisted: why should I give up what I ought to own, and what I've really prepared for all these past years?

Donald sat in his car until long after dark. That evening he ate dinner alone in the Ottimista, a wine bar near his apartment on Union Street because the atmosphere of the place seemed right to do the serious thinking he required to consider a restructuring of his life.

Hours later, when he attempted to sleep, he tossed and turned until his bed looked like a hurricane had blown through it. During the night, he slipped out of bed, took out a ballpoint pen and wrote a letter.

* * *

At ten o'clock in the morning a clean, newly-painted tanker truck followed Marco's pickup onto the *Dancing Horse* property. The driver, a tall, thin man with a completely shaved head and an air of confidence, climbed down from the cab. Marco stepped out of his own vehicle and motioned for the driver to follow him on into the winery.

They both stopped outside of Anna's office. Marco poked his head in. "Anna, where's your father?"

"He's away somewhere. I didn't ask."

"Well," Marco explained, "Joseph asked me to help him sell your bulk wine."

"So now you're a *negociant.* Why don't you move to France? I hear there are good opportunities for your kind over there."

Not too long ago she had given him a fine compliment, now she was back with her cynicism. "Just cool it," he said. "We don't need your scorn today." He nodded toward the driver. "This is Justin Jones. I believe he knows who you are."

"Actually, I know you also, Justin. I can't quite place you though."

"I worked at the Sutter Home Winery for a while. Now I'm a full partner with the V.I.P. Wines Company."

"That explains it. You shaved your head. Looks good on you."

"Thanks."

Marco wondered whether Anna was flirting with the man or just being irritable. He ignored her attitude. "Justin is here to test your batch. I believe it was left in the old tank after you restarted the fermenting with a more traditional yeast. You look surprised, Anna. Didn't your father tell you we had talked?"

"Yes. I wasn't aware you knew so much about the status of our operation and that you would bring someone around quite so soon."

"Do want to sell the lot or not?"

"Of course. It's for sale."

"Then let's get started."

"Are you the same Marco I used to know? You're so decisive, all business, no pleasant conversation."

"I can thank you for that."

Because of the other man present, Anna repressed her next comment.

Justin had been listening to the banter and began to feel uncomfortable. "Ms. Pugliesi, if there is something wrong with the wine, or if you don't want this deal to go through, please let me know. I'll be on my way."

"No," Anna protested. "Marco and I have a bumpy history. I want to sell the contents of that tank. Let me pull out a sample for you and see what you think. Follow me."

When they walked outside on the way up to the stainless steel tanks, Anna saw the large truck parked near the building. "What sort of truck is that? Not an oil tanker, I hope."

"No, of course not," Justin laughed. "This was once a milk carrier. We had to clean it thoroughly and sanitize the interior of the tank, and then we repainted the outside blue and silver. How do you like it?"

"As well as I could like a truck, I guess. Can you transport wine in there?"

"You can store wine in this tank as you do in your fermentation tanks. We just don't have refrigeration or heat. Once we load our cargo, I drive immediately to our facility where we unload. Then our technicians finish off, blend, filter, ferment or even barrel-age the load, whatever we decide is needed to make the wine ready for bottling."

Justin sampled the wine Anna offered him. Before giving her an analysis, he called his partner on the cell phone. "Kind of raw," he explained. "Has a good nose and the beginning of firm tannin, light acidity. We could work with this. If we use it for a base and blend it with that Malbec or maybe the Merlot we bought last week, I think we'll have a saleable product." He waited to hear his partner's remarks over the phone and then turned his attention to Anna.

She had an almost startling look when she asked, "Do you really believe you can make this drinkable? How is that possible?"

"It's possible if we do what a lot of wineries do: something that is not a secret, but I'm sure you would never try."

"And what in the world are you talking about?"

"In addition to blending, we're going to add a concentrate of grape juice to sweeten the wine before selling it. Will this make a difference in your decision?"

"No, I guess not, if it's legal."

"Good. We'll take the whole batch, probably need to make two trips with my portable tanker." An easy smile came to his face.

"You made that decision very fast," Anna said. "Makes me wonder if I'm doing the right thing by selling."

Marco cut in, "Now that's not the Anna I know, the one who knows it all and never questions her own thoughts."

She glared at him but this time suppressed making a comment.

Marco didn't let up: "I think perhaps it's time you returned control of the winemaking to your father. He knows what he's doing, and you're proving to be an insecure amateur."

Anna ignored him and spoke directly to Justin: "Mr. Jones, come into my office when you finish loading here. We'll settle the account." She didn't wait for his answer, just strode off and into the stone building.

Marco guided Justin as he drove the tanker up on the level close to the old fourth steel tank. He helped him connect a line from the tank and waited while half the wine was pumped in to fill the tanker. He then went with Justin into Anna's office.

Anna had the invoice ready. Justin agreed with her price, wrote her a check and said, "I'll return for the rest of the batch in a few hours. Nice doing business with you." He shook hands and held Anna's hand a moment longer than might have been necessary for a business transaction. Her enigmatic smile left him wondering.

Marco stayed in the office after Justin left.

"Why are you still here?" Anna asked.

"Not because I expect any thanks from you."

"Well, I appreciate what you've done. Is that what you want to hear?"

"No," Marco explained patiently. "Something I have to tell you. You caught my curiosity when you asked if I'm a *negociant.* I'm going to attend the Vin Expo in Bordeaux next month."

"Congratulations! Why tell me about it?"

"Certainly not because I want you to come along."

"Why then?"

"Just drop the attitude for a minute and I'll let you know. I already talked this over with your father and he agrees. He wanted me to check with you. Don't say anything. Let me finish. I want to bring a dozen cases of your best wine. I'm renting a booth in the California exhibit where I'll be contacting restaurateurs, salespeople, sommeliers, winemakers, vignerons of all varieties. What do you think about my promoting your wines in Europe?"

"I don't know what to think about you any more, but, yes, I'd like to have our wine on display at the Expo. So I guess I'll have to thank you for that."

"You guess?" Marco said and shook his head in resignation. "Of course, I'll let you choose which wines to send. Will you have a new label ready by then?"

"I have some of the original drawings my grandmother made when she was designing the label for the Emma Mae Vineyard. They're very good. One has the vineyard in the background and a beautiful yearling colt moving across the foreground. I could use that one for now."

"Sounds good. I know an excellent printer."

"Never mind. I'll take care of that myself."

Marco had to laugh at her curt response as he walked away from the building.

* * *

The district attorney summoned Donald Stanton to her office for an interview. He drove across town, parked in an overpriced parking lot, and only had to wait outside the office for a nervous twenty minutes before being called in. A court-appointed very young defense attorney sat in on the meeting but might as well have not been there as far as Donald was concerned. The nondescript fellow hardly said a word, and seemed either afraid or in awe of the dominant woman in control of the proceeding.

The woman's short-cropped gray hair and fit athletic body, clothed in black, exuded a strong, determined character. The session, led by this stern non-smiling elected official doing most of the talking, lasted for forty-five minutes. Her questions were both direct and unavoidable. Donald answered as succinctly as possible, but did not at any point admit to doing anything wrong nor did he offer any additional information.

When asked directly if he started a fire in the Pugliesi barn, he turned to the novice attorney sitting beside him. "Do I have to answer that?"

"You should," the timid fellow said.

"But do I have to?"

"No one can force you, I guess." He looked at the D.A. for support. "Wouldn't that be answering under duress?" he asked her.

She glared at him and responded slowly through tightened jaw muscles, "No pressure will intentionally come from this office."

The D.A. glared at Stanton for a few moments and then signaled her disapproval of his tactics with a brief snort through her nostrils and then warned him not to leave the Bay area until she had finished with her investigation. She did inform him that charges had not yet been brought against him by the Pugliesi family, but that didn't preclude her from prosecuting him herself if she deemed it necessary.

Donald walked away from the meeting feeling extremely uncertain about his future. Back at the bank, no one asked so he explained to no one where he had been. That afternoon he decided he would mail the letter he had written earlier to Anna.

* * *

Two days later when the letter reached Anna, she waited as usual for evening before reading her personal mail. When she saw the return address, she nearly ripped it into strips without glancing at the contents. Strangely enough she controlled her anger, tore the envelope open using a finger like a dull knife and then sat back to find out why someone she detested would write to her.

> Dear Anna,
>
> I want very much to speak with you. I don't know if you will respond, but I have to try. I'm not proud of any of my recent covert activities. You have good reason to hate and shun me, and I can't blame you for that.
>
> First of all I want you to know that I'm contemplating relinquishing all claims to your winery and property. Grandfather made no claims on either, and I probably shouldn't have come to the conclusion which I did. I believe your assessment might be right. He and your grandmother were youngsters caught up in the madness during World War Two. If they had stayed together, it likely would not have worked out anyhow.
>
> I respect your father, their child, who didn't deserve the treatment I gave him. Your father is a genuinely good person, and so was his half-brother, my father, who is gone now and so, I regret, is my mother. I was their only child. So except for your family, I have no relatives with whom I can communicate. My attitude toward other people has not brought on any lasting friends. In retrospect I see how my whole

approach to life and its myriad potential has been a disaster. I even might have to serve time for some of my actions. If so, I will hold no one else responsible.

If you can somehow bring yourself to contact me or meet me somewhere sometime, I want to make both personal and financial things right between us. R.S.V.P.

Sincerely,
Donald Stanton

Anna astonished by the contents, read the letter once more, sat back and nearly screamed. She held her head between her hands and uttered a deep moan. She took the letter in hand, left her section of the house and went looking for her father. He was sitting in his easy chair where she knew he would be reading the *San Francisco Chronicle*. She handed him the letter with no explanation.

Joseph read it twice, then said, "Why don't you tear it up?"

"I'm not sure. There is a sense of openness in the letter combined with a desperate plea for help. I can't just dismiss him without considering what he's saying."

"On the surface he's saying one thing, but under it he has another motive," Joseph pointed out. "Notice that he never named what covert activities he was involved in, nothing to indict himself. More than likely if he can soften you, he'll come around from another direction where he'll try again to squeeze control of the winery."

"I don't know." Anna countered. "He has admitted he's done things he's not proud of."

"A smoke screen. I don't trust him. Give the letter to Schmidt, the investigating officer. He might be able to use this as the evidence needed to indict Stanton and send him behind bars."

"That would be a low, mean, underhanded thing to do."

"He is all of those things and more. Is he offering to rebuild the barn, to replace our equipment, our new burnt-out tractor?"

Anna shook her head, retrieved the letter and said, "Don't do anything or tell anyone about this just yet, Dad. I have to mull this over for a while." She walked soberly to her rooms where she slumped into a chair and eventually phoned her friend Chip Calahan.

"I have a dilemma in my life, Chip. I want to tell you about it, but first you must promise me not to speak with anyone about what I say."

"No problem, Anna. What's going on?"

"Not on the phone. Could we meet tomorrow? I'll drive to the city if you can't come up this way."

"Actually I can't be away from work for too long. We are in contract negotiations with two new players and their intractable agents. I would be able to break loose for about an hour to meet you with for lunch if you like."

"That would be fine, Chip. See you tomorrow then?" she asked. He agreed, so they chose to meet at the old Cliff House restaurant where they could look out over the ocean while discussing her concerns.

Anna arrived first and told the hostess she would wait for her friend. When she saw Chip coming up the steps, she realized she'd forgotten how handsome he was. His head of curly hair had been trimmed down giving him a neat, young executive look. He wore a beige sports coat with a blue shirt open at the collar. His gait was casual, his manner maybe a bit self-absorbed, his smile ready and engaging. When they greeted, Anna surprised herself by giving Chip a long warm embrace, showing more affection than she had to anyone in a long time.

"Nice to see you," he said as he pulled away not responding at all to her demonstration.

"How are those negotiations coming along?" she asked.

"Painful. Quarterbacks are the prima donnas of modern football. We desperately need a franchise player but could do without the attitude this one throws around."

"You said two players. How about the other?"

"A defensive lineman, solid, family man. No character problems there, just wants more money than it originally cost to build the stadium."

An attractive young lady showed them to a table with a view that had Anna looking out at the Pacific while Chip watched the girl walking away from the table with hip-moving, subtle undulations.

"If I could have your attention, Chip, I really do need your advice."

"Oh, sorry. Of course, I was just distracted for a moment there."

"So I noticed."

"You said you had a dilemma?"

"I still do." She noticed now that Chip was looking out over the water, and his mind seemed to be somewhere out there, too. She opened the menu and noticed he still stared vacantly toward the horizon. When a waiter showed up, food seemed unimportant to her, so she just asked for the daily special.

Chip broke away from his thoughts for a moment and ordered the first thing he saw on the menu, then went back into a hibernation mode with his own problems.

Anna was content to sit quietly and think for a while. She questioned herself as to whether talking with a lawyer was really the right thing to do. Why had she called for this meeting? After all, she wasn't planning to bring legal action against Stanton.

She was also acutely aware that Chip hadn't returned any feeling in that first encounter. How someone goes about giving a hug can tell a great deal about that person's feeling. She wondered if perhaps she had wanted to see him for personal reasons which had nothing to do with solving her dilemma. She was quickly coming to the conclusion that this meeting was a mistake, so she asked a question which might have come off like a non-sequitur, except there was something she wanted to learn about Chip before taking him into her confidence. "How is that pretty girl you brought to our winery party? Are you still seeing her?"

"Ah . . . no," he said. "I've moved on. I found someone even prettier."

"Oh, and is she perhaps more intelligent than the previous one?"

"I guess so. I don't know. We don't talk about much. Well, actually we don't talk about anything at all. If you know what I mean?"

"I'm beginning to understand."

"What was it you wanted to see me about?"

"I was thinking I needed help concerning a legal problem, but now I believe it's more of a personal nature and really ought to remain a family matter. Sorry about taking you away from your job this way. I think we should just have a good lunch, my treat, and I'll work things out for myself."

"That's okay by me. I wanted an excuse to get away from those sharks for a while. By the way, if you're interested, I can get you tickets for any of our home games."

"No, thanks, Chip. Football is the furthest thing from my mind right now."

The food came. They enjoyed the seascape and shook hands as they parted, still friends but certainly not with any hint of romance.

Anna decided while she was in the city, she would confront Stanton himself. She thought perhaps a face to face might give her a clue about his intentions and therefore help solve her dilemma. She attempted to drive across town to get to the Central Bank. The traffic was far worse than she remembered. Unfortunately she had neglected to turn on the radio for the traffic report. While she was having lunch, a truck missed the on-ramp to the 101, rolled over onto one side with its cargo of high-octane gasoline. The metal sliding on the concrete threw out sparks that ignited several thousand gallons of fuel, leaving most of the city from Interstate 280 to Golden Gate Park in a snarl of machinery, horns, tempers, and sirens.

Later in the day Donald Stanton was startled into semi-shock to see Anna walking into his office. At first he couldn't speak, and she didn't make it any easier for him. She seated herself and waited for him to say something.

Finally he recovered enough to say, "I wasn't prepared for you to walk in on me."

"You shouldn't have to prepare. If what you said in your letter was sincere, you can start with that."

"Yes. Somehow, I want to do whatever I can to make things right with us."

"Somehow is far too vague. You can't undo what you've already done. Why aren't you in jail right now?"

Donald looked around hoping no one in the adjoining offices could overhear their conversation. "No action has been taken against me. I had to meet with the district attorney. She said they were investigating; so far all evidence is circumstantial. I assume you haven't yet filed charges or I would no doubt be behind bars."

"Why don't you just admit your involvement?"

"I can't do that, at least not to the authorities. I'm trying to change my life around. I realize not everyone who's done wrong has a chance like this. Everything I said in the letter is true. I'm not proud of what I've done. I want to make things right if you'll give me that opportunity."

"Hey, don't hang the onus on me. I'm not your savior. I'm not even sure coming here was the right thing to do."

Donald sat quietly for a long time.

Anna stared at him and was herself wondering how she should proceed. "My father thought I should tear up your letter. He doesn't trust you and is opposed to anything you might suggest. I wonder if maybe I should just go along with him. He believes you have another agenda, and you will try again to gain control of our winery."

Donald opened the central drawer on his desk and pulled out a sheaf of papers. "I have been redrafting your father's loan. I lowered the interest rate and am allowing him an extended period to make those payments. I would underwrite it myself, but then I'm sure he would think I have an ulterior motive."

Anna read the policy. "I don't know what to say."

He handed the draft to her. "If you will give him that copy, I would appreciate it."

"At this point, I'm not sure I care what you appreciate."

"But you did come here, and I know that wasn't easy. I understand the traffic in town today is a nightmare."

"The traffic is nothing compared to the turmoil I've been going through internally."

"Anna, I regret making you suffer. Tell you what I'd like to do. Will you let me replace some of the equipment lost in the fire? At least some of the items not covered by insurance."

Anna saw a look on his face which came on but quickly vanished: the look was a momentary smugness as though he had won a small skirmish. She asked skeptically, "How do you know we have insurance?"

"When the bank writes a loan, we investigate. The tractor is fully covered. Many of the tools and loose items are not. I could help you with those."

"What about the old barn itself? They are becoming scarce, irreplaceable, and on the personal level my Chardonnay cuttings!!! I had plans for those clones next season."

"I don't know how to replace the cuttings. The barn was ancient. You'll get some aid but not much there. How would you like a new prefab storage facility? They're available and easy to install. I could assist you with securing your insurance coverage on that type of building."

Anna put her head in her hands. "You talk a good story, Donald, but I don't know where it's leading. I think I just need to get out of here and think things through." She pushed her chair back and started toward the door.

Donald stood up, but before he could say a word, she said, "No, don't say anything more. I'll show this draft to my father. That's all I can promise. Goodbye!"

* * *

Joseph listened with great skepticism as Anna recounted her visit with Donald Stanton. He responded, holding back as much emotion as he could. "After all he's done, I couldn't conceive of him as a nephew. A charlatan, a hustler, an arsonist maybe, but certainly not a member of the family."

"What about the rewritten loan contract? It appears straightforward, genuine."

"Anna, you haven't acquired too many faults as you were growing into maturity. I never thought being naïve would now become one of them. This is nothing but a draft. It's not signed by Arbuthnot or any of the bank's executives."

"Oh, Dad, I admit, I'm not at all sure what to do about him. There's a slickness about him in his manner or smile. I can't pin it down."

"I don't trust the man."

"Do you believe the story that he is related to us?"

"I suppose there's some truth to it," Joseph conceded. "If it were not for your grandmother, I might have carried the surname Stanton. Still that doesn't give him the right to undermine us. His grandfather had nothing to do with the winery. He never worked here nor was ever any part of it."

"Of course not, but if Donald actually is family . . ."

"Anna, you have a family, and you could start having more family if you wanted."

"You mean, with Marco?"

Joseph nodded, but chose to say nothing more about that.

CHAPTER 13

Marco flew to Paris, and from there caught a short flight to Bordeaux with a case of *Dancing Horse* wines sent on ahead of him. His booth at the Vin Expo began quietly with only a few vintners showing mild interest in his display. Finally an American journalist he'd met once and read frequently stopped by and asked to sample the Emma Mae Cabernet Sauvignon.

The wine writer, a gray shaggy-haired hulk of man, who had a strong following in both Europe and the States, sampled the Cabernet and left with a thoughtful look, but offered no comment. In his daily notes, circulated at the Expo and published on his website, he praised the Emma Mae Cabernet as full-bodied, well-balanced, and more satisfying than the French equivalent and so awarded it a 94-point rating. Several sommeliers and distributors quickly moved in to sample the wine. A couple of them even promised to place orders when they returned home.

One of the sommeliers, a most attractive girl, approached the booth. Her hair was dark and cropped close to her head, her eyes sky-blue, a figure lean with curves in just the right places. At first Marco thought she was about nineteen or so, but when she spoke to him, her maturity and manner made him realize she was perhaps twenty-nine or thirty.

She introduced herself using only her last name, DiSantis, and told him that she was employed by a Parisian restaurant as a sommelier.

"Do you have a first name?"

"Of course, it's Pookie. Does that strike you as strange or unusual?"

"Not strange, perhaps unusual, but I see there's a lot about you that's unusual and interesting."

Pookie returned the second and third day with Marco encouraging her as she sampled a different variety each time. On the fourth day, the slim, dark-haired girl shook his hand and held it gently against her breast, then asked Marco quite frankly, "Will I also get to sample you?"

After closing the booth for the evening, the young lady took him by the arm, led him to a restaurant she knew which opened onto the large walking zone in Bordeaux and later across that zone and on to her room at the St. Catherine Hotel.

When they entered the room, Marco made no move toward Pookie. He studied the décor and said, "Soft lights, pink walls and red carpets, very impressive, as are you. I've never seen a hotel quite like this or met anyone quite like you."

"Is that bad?"

"Why no, just an observation."

Pookie DiSantis, rather than having a French accent, spoke English with a distinct Cockney flavor. "I wonder about you Americans. Are you all so reticent?" She pulled Marco down onto the firm, wide bed where she helped him overcome a few preliminary inhibitions. His inhibitions came because he questioned whether he would be untrue to Anna if he had an affair with this sommelier. At least he wasn't interested just so he could sell wine. That would have been crass. She was a most attractive young woman, and he had suffered a long drought because of Anna's refusal to decide their future or to let him stay with her. Well, he had never planned to remain celibate. Though he was surprised at himself, Marco did not resist very long, the girl or himself.

They spent a marvelously sensuous evening, resumed the following night and the one after that, which was the day before Marco was planning to leave for California.

Except for Pookie's desire for sex, which was insatiable, or maybe because of it, Marco quickly grew extremely fond of her. In addition to her lithe figure, she was witty, intelligent, had a thorough knowledge of wine, was quick to laugh, and even quicker to poke fun at him when he indicated they probably should not be spending so much time together.

Marco suggested he didn't know where this tryst was going. She said, "Don't labor over it, love. Like drinking good wine, life is here to enjoy."

He relaxed and stopped resisting as he almost did the first night, but he still couldn't understand or completely accept this total abandonment to passion. Pookie made no demands on him. Since she was unlike any woman he had ever known, that made him even less confident about her possible motives.

"You know I'll be leaving tomorrow. I'm not sure when I'll see you again."

"Oh, don't be sad about it. Haven't you rather enjoyed our time together?"

"Definitely. You've introduced to me a world I've never before experienced."

"I find you a very passionate yet sensitive man. Let us not say goodbye. Instead of taking the plane from Bordeaux, tomorrow drive with me to Paris. We can spend a few more days together. Would you like that?"

* * *

Marco and Pookie didn't get to Paris the next day, but he did call the airline to postpone and change his flight. Driving her Mini Cooper slowly along the coast, they stayed one night in the industrial city of Nantes on the Loire River, and another in the smaller town of Chartres just southwest of Paris. Though they might have completed the journey to Paris earlier if either had felt any reason to hurry, instead they visited the ancient Gothic Cathedral, sampled wine in several wine bars, and then visited each other.

The following day in Paris, Pookie introduced Marco to the staff at her restaurant on the Left Bank with a view to Notre Dame. She assured him she would order his *Dancing Horse* wines. She explained that she supposed not too many of the French would buy the wine, but visiting Americans would delight in drinking it because that was a way of getting back at the arrogant Frenchmen who disdained drinking those terrible American wines.

The two only spent one night at Pookie's apartment located at the upper end of the Champs-Elysees near the Arc de Triomphe where she said the shopping was sensational. Marco took her word for that but said he'd rather go up the Eiffel Tower to experience the extraordinary view, which they did.

In the morning, when Pookie dropped Marco off at the Orley International Airport, she kissed him lightly on the lips and said, "I can't promise when I might come to your lovely California, but you do know where I live now. Don't stay away too long."

On the long flight home, Marco realized he'd really been on quite a journey with this liberated French girl, but certainly didn't know if he'd actually gotten anywhere emotionally with her, or whether any of his experiences would alter his feelings about Anna. Somehow he wanted to see Anna more than ever but also wondered about their relationship, as if anything could possibly have changed between them.

* * *

Donald Stanton had been busy in his own way, reading newspaper articles whenever he could find them about wine and winemaking. Usually they were in the food section of the *San Francisco Chronicle* and the *Examiner*. He also purchased a couple of wine magazines, reading them with the intention of learning more about the world of wine.

In one he found an article which piqued his interest. He'd read that an insect, which is native to the southeastern states and feeds mostly in citrus and avocado groves, had carried a devastating disease to the California almond groves. Unfortunately for grape growers, the glassy-winged sharpshooter also feeds on dormant grape vines. It's an extremely ugly, half-inch long, dark brown bug that flies with transparent wings and carries Pierce's disease to the vegetation it inhabits. The bacteria blocks the plant's vessels from carrying water and nutrients within itself; leaves become dry or scorched, vines begin to die in a year or two.

Donald soon figured how this information might help him in his quest. He wondered how someone might go about securing a gaggle of these little sharpshooters.

* * *

As soon as the jet landed and he could turn on his cell phone, Marco called Anna declaring he would like to have a meeting with her and told her he would be over to see her soon.

"You back from Europe? Why didn't you stay? You should know you're not wanted here."

"Now you can't mean that."

"You left me alone at a party with guests who expected you to be there. You respond by sending me a telegram, letting me explain something I could not explain."

"That was a direct result of your indecision. If you wanted me in your life, you would have let me know. I saw no reason to be at the party since there was nothing I could have said that would make any difference."

"You should have had more patience."

"Well, I'm calling now because I have some news about successfully selling your wine in France, and I was hoping somehow we might at least be civil to each other."

"Come over if you wish, but don't expect me to have any trumpets announcing your arrival."

"No, I know what to expect, or I should say what not to expect from you. I'll be there in the morning."

"I'll wave a French flag."

Marco hung up without retaliating. About midmorning he showed up in her lab with an armful of flowers and a contract for her to sign for a fair-sized shipment of Emma Mae Vineyard Cabernet and a few cases of Chardonnay.

"Where do these go?" she asked. "I don't see a business name, just a restaurant in Paris."

"That's right. This order will go to my friend who is the sommelier in that restaurant."

"A restaurant and not a major distributor? A single sommelier doesn't sound like a much of an inroad."

"I've made several contacts with distributors who showed interest in your wines and will probably place orders, but this is the first solid contact."

"I see. So who is this man? Does he have a name?"

"The sommelier is not a man, but a woman, and a most attractive one at that."

"How lucky for you," Anna scoffed. "Were you also lucky with her?"

"Why would you care? You seem to have no personal interest in me."

"You did then, didn't you?"

"Would that bother you if I did?"

Anna hesitated before saying, "Why should it?"

"Maybe it shouldn't, but since you're asking, it seems to me you're already making something out of it."

"I don't want to get into this with you." She threw her hands in the air, waving both palms outward in a gesture of shaking off the matter.

Just then, Steve, the cooper's handsome son, stuck his head in the office. "Anything else you want me to do, Miss Pugliesi?"

"Yes, Steve. Study this order. I'd like you to box this wine so Mr. Preziano may ship it out for me."

"Hi, Mr. Preziano." He shook Marco's hand. "We missed you at the party. Do you like the new name for the winery?"

"As a matter of fact I do," Marco said as Steve walked out reading the shipping order.

"Too young for you," Marco said as soon as Steve was out of the office. "I see you've been socially active yourself." He couldn't contain a smile.

Anna realized he was needling her, but still she overreacted. "He's Freddie's assistant, not mine. Don't try to make any more out of it than that."

"Wouldn't dream of it, but then he is a good-looking young man and you certainly didn't hesitate taking him on when he asked you."

"Don't be ridiculous." Anna felt the need to explain. "You already know Steve wants to learn the wine business, but, of course, you are always away and haven't given him any of your time or advice." She paused and then continued, "Besides he is very interested in Freddie's other helper, our attractive apprentice Leticia."

"Are you sure? Working around you, he might become more attracted to an older woman."

"Will you please leave now?"

"Certainly. Do you want a visitor tonight?"

That caught her off guard. "No, of course not. Remember you are the one who called a stop to those visits."

"That was to give you time to make up your mind, which you never did."

"I don't want to get into that right now. I've asked you to leave."

Marco didn't leave because he had earlier thought out something important he wanted to tell her, so he just began speaking: "When Odysseus returned home after his travels, he found several suitors with his wife Penelope, not that she was interested in any of them."

"What are you talking about?"

"When I lived with you, I thought that was home. Now I feel like Homer's Odysseus. I have been wandering for years trying to get back home to you."

"You've gotten me confused. You travel, get lost or whatever happened in Europe, found temptation, and now want to return home. Odysseus never had it so good."

"At least Penelope let him know she wanted him back."

"Will you just go away and let me think things through?"

Marco gave out an exasperated sigh as he left. He was hoping his story about having found a home with her might get Anna to reconsider what their relationship could be. He was certainly sincere about his intent. Now all he could feel was her uncertainty and his frustration.

* * *

Donald Stanton tried two things to ingratiate himself with Anna. He emailed her the drawings he had Xeroxed from a magazine for a new modern-designed storage shed to go on the site where the barn used to be. The structure was to be upscale: two long buildings with a covered walkway between them. Each side could be sectioned off depending on its usage.

Anna remained skeptical yet somewhat favorably impressed with the drawings.

Stanton also added that he had prompted her insurance agent to shortcut the paperwork necessary to release the funds for the purchase of a new tractor for the winery.

Later in the week, Joseph saw a flatbed truck loaded with what looked like a brand new, green and white John Deere tractor. The carrier truck stopped off the highway adjacent to the property entrance. He watched as a man climbed out of the passenger side of the truck and then struggled up onto the tractor. The truck driver lowered the flat tailgate and then stood off to one side so he could guide the man who carefully backed the tractor off the truck. Joseph then realized who was driving the tractor. As the man was wearing jeans and a denim shirt, he did not at first recognize Stanton. He shook his head to get the image out of his mind and went immediately into the winery to warn Anna.

"He's here already?" she asked. "I knew he was coming. Donald informed me by email, and I agreed to accept his offer."

"So that means he's admitting responsibility for burning our barn."

"He never admitted anything, just said he wants to see us succeed."

"Damn! I don't trust that creep for a second."

"You know the insurance is paying for the tractor. Donald just acted as facilitator. He's also going to have a modern storage shed built for us to replace the barn. He sent me the plans. It's very nice, and he seems willing to pay for that. So how bad can he be?"

"If he wants us to succeed, it is merely because he thinks it will all be his eventually. You can go out to greet him. If I go, I'm sure I'd tell him what he can do with his plans and his tractor." Joseph pressed his fist against his mouth while his eyes glared hostility.

"Dad, I've never seen you show so much anger."

"That man is poison. When a scorpion strikes, it doesn't lose its stinger. It can strike again at any time."

"Okay, so I won't invite him to stay over for lunch, but he seems sincere enough to me."

"I never realized you could be so naïve."

"Well, Dad, he is almost family. Shouldn't we at least give him a chance?"

"Your soft side could get you in trouble." Joseph whirled away and strode into the house.

Anna went outside to greet Stanton who exuded a strange smile that either hid something or showed he was overly pleased with himself. She inspected the tractor, which appeared to be brand new, but couldn't decipher the strange look on his face.

"How do you like the tractor?"

"I like it fine. Is it legal?"

"It's legal and it comes free and clear. Where do you want me to park it?"

"Put it behind the house near the old cabins."

"That where the Chinese used to live?"

"Yes, and the Mexicans, and whoever else comes to work during harvest season and pruning time and whenever we need help."

He pulled the tractor around to where she suggested and handed her the paid receipt he'd been given with the tractor. "Don't believe I'll ask for the opportunity to stay in one of those cabins. Your father is not too pleased with me, is he?"

"Do you blame him?"

"Given the circumstances, no. You'll find out I'm going to make up for all the lost time between us." He glanced over to see where the truck was parked near the entrance. "I see the driver is still waiting to give me a ride back to town. Let's keep in touch."

Stanton ran awkwardly down the driveway, too self-conscious and satisfied with himself to be relaxed.

Anna watched him and then turned her attention inward to her concerns about what kind of man he truly was. Though she often disagreed with her father, she couldn't easily dismiss his doubts regarding Stanton. Perhaps she was being naïve, but right now she couldn't solve that quandary. She had more important business regarding her winery.

Examining the Chardonnay that had been moved earlier to the redwood, she determined it was as good as it would ever be and ready for bottling. She then asked her father if he thought it was ready to bottle. He readily agreed so she called Federica to ask if she could get her assistants to help with the bottling, and if she would be certain to let the lees remain in the cask and not be pumped out with the wine.

Federica loved this part of the winemaking process even better than using the press. She could see the liquid, this time the clean, aromatic white Chardonnay, filling each bottle.

"Anna, are you going to try synthetic corks this time? I know you've been considering it."

"No, I think we'll stay with traditional methods. The synthetics don't always seal properly, and we can't afford to lose any more wine this year with my foolish experiments."

The following day, Federica brought in her two assistants, Leticia and Steve, and showed Steve what Scott had taught her in order to get the bottling machine to cooperate.

Federica siphoned the wine carefully from the cask. She knew what Anna meant so was careful not to allow the sediment to come up with the wine. Steve proved to be adept with mechanics so he operated all the phases of the bottling machine, being sure the bottles lined up properly and that corks were set firmly into each bottle. Leticia opened the fresh packages of cork, feeding them and the new 750-ml bottles as needed into the apparatus, and then carried the crisp clear bottles of wine to the central storage tunnel placing them in racks rising against the walls.

The day after the Chardonnay had been bottled and stored for further aging, a flatbed truck carrying a walk-in metallic box measuring ten by twelve by eight arrived. Two muscular men wearing grey T-shirts with *Oxy Construction* printed on the back slowly got out of the truck. One of the two ambled into the winery to seek Anna.

"I got something outside for you. You wanna let me know where to drop it off?"

"Let's go out and have a look." Outside she saw a pale yellow box on the truck. "What is that?"

"Well, it's a storage shed, lady; full opening, double-door front."

"Where is the rest of it? I was promised a prefab storage facility with two long buildings and a roof connecting them."

"I don't know anything about two buildings. We don't own the company; we only work for it. This is what we were told to deliver. You want it or not?"

Anna thought for only a moment. "Go ahead, drop it off. I'll deal with the perpetrator later."

"The what?"

"Never mind."

"Where do you want it to go?"

"Up there on that flat area where the barn used to be. I guess Donald Stanton is not a man of his word."

"Pardon?"

"Forget it. Just drop the thing off on the closest corner where you see the burnt remains of a building."

One man drove the truck up to the barn site, the other directed him to back into the corner. He pulled a lever that activated the hydraulics, lowering the rear of the flatbed. The edge of the steel box slid down to the ground and the truck slowly pulled forward leaving the storage box standing upright, a sad replacement for a once classic red barn.

"Sign this if you will."

Anna signed the invoice and the truck pulled away. About that time Joseph came out to see what was going on.

"Dad, I think you were dead-on right about Stanton. This is our new storage shed. It's supposed to replace a double prefabricated state-of-the-art storage facility."

"Sitting out here," Joseph observed, "it looks like a lonely orphan. It doesn't fit with anything on the property. Why did you accept it?"

"Well, the sudden delivery kind of blindsided me, but I think it will be useful. The front doors swing all the way open. We need someplace to store the tractor, and we have a few tools that survived the fire."

"So Stanton thinks you'll accept crumbs when he promises filet?"

CHAPTER 14

Scott Anderson started early in the morning and had been working late up in Santa Rosa. By the time he finished installing and then testing a new centrifuge filter, it was nearly midnight. The owner wanted to write a check for him right then, but Scott said he was too tired. He could wait for morning to the settle the bill. "Rest means more to me right now than money."

As the Valley rested peacefully in the dark night sky, Scott drove home. On his way he had to pass by the Pugliesi vineyards. He slowed to a stop, turned off his headlights, and got out of the pickup to check out the newly posted sign over the driveway entrance. He could tell it was a laser-etched flat of hardwood. Even in the darkness, Scott could make out the shadow of a magnificently carved stallion. Both the neck and tail were arched in frozen motion, one knee raised preparing to tap hoof to earth. No words had been inscribed on the board, simply the carving to let the passing world know what was behind the equestrian logo.

Scott admired the sign, nodded his approval, and was ready to continue on home but saw another shadow moving about out in the vineyards.

Whoever was out there was so absorbed in what he was doing that he hadn't noticed Scott's truck slow to a stop in front of the property. The person was carrying a small cardboard box and was flinging handfuls of its contents onto the dormant grape vines in the Emma Mae Vineyard.

Scott walked through the dark toward the busy figure. It appeared to Scott that the person was throwing some live insects at the rows of vines. When he was close enough, he shouted out, "What are you doing?"

Startled, Stanton whirled around. At first he could only stare and say nothing, then, still holding his box, began running toward the highway.

Scott easily caught him, tackled him, and whipped his body to the ground. With a knee on the intruder's back, he said, "You're Donald Stanton, aren't you? I've been hearing about you. What do you have in that box?"

"Hey! Let me up. Who the hell do you think you are?"

"No. You'll answer the questions here." Scott looked into the box. "Damned, these are those glassy-winged-something insects I've read about. You're spreading these on the Pugliesi's vines? You bastard!"

"What's it to you? This is rightly my vineyard. I can do whatever I want."

"The hell you can! Let's go up to the house. Find out what Anna and Joseph think about this."

"I'm not going anywhere with you." Stanton struggled to his feet and tried to get away, but Scott was far too strong for him. He grabbed Donald's hand, twisted it around behind him, then picked up the box and pushed Donald toward the house.

"All right, all right," Donald said. "How much do you want? What'll it take to let me go?"

"Shut up, and just keep walking."

"I'll pay you whatever you want. Just let me go."

"The best thing for you right now is to shut your mouth and keep walking."

"Who the hell are you anyhow? Why do you care what I do on my own property?"

Holding the cardboard box under one arm, Scott pushed Donald along keeping his arm bent behind him until they came to the rear of the house. He set the box down. Then with one hand still holding his captive, he used the free one to pound on the door while shouting, "Anna! Joseph! Wake up! Do you hear me? It's Scott. Wake up!"

Soon lights came on in the back yard. Anna came out from her bedroom door wearing a bathrobe and slippers. Joseph exited from the main house rear door. They saw Scott holding Stanton. Perplexed, they both waited for an explanation.

"Look in this box," Scott said. "This creep was spreading these on your vines."

Anna opened the box and knew instantly what it contained. "Glassy-winged sharpshooters! They carry Pierce's disease. Why you dirty bastard. They'll kill the vines." She completely lost her temper and lunged at Donald grabbing him by the throat with both hands.

Joseph had to pry his daughter's fingers from the man's throat. "Don't kill him, Anna. You'll only make matters worse."

She allowed her father to pull her hands away, but she dragged her fingernails slicing through the skin on both sides of his throat. "I've never felt so much like throttling someone as I do this creep."

"You don't want ending his life on your record."

"How can you stay calm at a time like this?"

"Honey, I'm not calm. I'm boiling inside, but I know this is not the time to lose control." He turned to Scott. "Can you hold him while I call the police?"

"Glad to."

When Joseph went inside, Anna closed the cardboard box as tightly as she could. She hissed at Stanton, "I guess my father was right about you all the time." She turned to Scott. "Did this parasite get many of the insects onto our vines?"

"I think so, Anna. He was spreading them for a while before I reached him."

Donald thought he'd better try saying something. "Ahh, let me explain something here."

Anna scoffed, "Just shut up! There's nothing for you to explain. You're caught, and you will pay for this."

Donald really didn't have an explanation thought out, so he kept quiet; but his mind was racing for a solution.

Joseph came out with a small piece of electrical cord which he used to quickly tie Donald's hands behind him. "Police are on the way."

"Good! Watch him for a minute. I'll be right back." Anna went into her bedroom and came out with some newspaper and matches. She crumpled the paper, set the cardboard box on top of the paper and lit the stack on fire.

"Don't want to let any more of these deadly insects getting out onto our vines," she explained.

As the flames came up the sides and quickly ignited the dry cardboard, the box and its contents crackled in the blaze. Donald smiled because he saw in the flames something he figured might help him get out of this predicament.

Soon two black-and-whites arrived. Anna tried to explain what had happened, but she was so keyed up she spoke too fast; no one could follow her.

Joseph intervened. "Perhaps you'd better let Scott explain what he saw."

Surprisingly Anna agreed, so Scott took his time to describe what he had witnessed.

One of the officers asked, "Are you sure this is the man you saw spreading the insects on the vines?"

"Positive. I walked him back to the house myself."

Donald was read the Miranda. He neither confirmed nor denied any involvement, nor did he attempt to explain anything about his actions. He was quickly cuffed and carted off in a police cruiser.

"We have to stop those insects from spreading," Anna said.

"What can we possibly do?" Joseph asked.

Out of desperation, Anna's brain was running at full speed. "I have an idea which just might work."

Without having to ask, Joseph's eyebrows arched in question.

"You know how vines were grafted onto root stock to save our industry from phylloxera? Well, I'm going to reverse that process."

"How is that possible?"

Anna answered without hesitation, "I'm going to cut off every plant that contains the insects right down to a few inches above the earth."

"Don't you think we'd better wait till morning? You won't be able to see what you are doing until we get some light."

"I'll have plenty of light. If you'll get me a machete, I want to get to work right now."

"We don't have such a tool on this estate," Joseph said.

"I think I can help with this," Scott offered.

"Do you have a machete with you?"

"No, but I have a chain saw at home. I'll get there and back as soon as possible."

"Anna, can't it just wait till morning?" Joseph asked. "The insects won't multiply overnight."

"No, but they can fly from one vine to another. Do you think I'd be able to sleep? Do you think I want to sleep while the Emma Mae Vineyard is being destroyed? I'll be out here cutting off as many vines as I can by hand before Scott returns. Why don't you call Oscar? Wake him up and ask him to hurry out here to help us collect these contaminated vines. We have to start a fire and burn them before they spread any farther. Ask Oscar if he has a chain saw. We need all the help we can get."

While Joseph used his cell phone to do what she asked, Anna ran off to their tool shed and returned with two carpenter saws.

"Here." She handed one to her father. "Let's cut away the worst of these plants first and stack them in a pile so we can burn them."

Joseph saw the sense in her solution, so he began sawing plants from the middle of the carnage. Anna worked next to him and carried armfuls of branches to form a stack near the center of the devastation. She grimaced and then set fire to the first pile of infected branches.

When Scott finally returned with the chain saw, he fired it up and headed to one side of the infected area. He began slicing off the vines near the base as Anna had suggested. He worked in a line on the extreme eastern edge of the infected plants. Joseph worked the other side with the conventional saw in a valiant attempt to rid the field of every sharpshooter. They boxed out the complete area and then began moving inward.

Anna broke from her cutting, followed the men gathering plants as she moved, and then returned to cut more vines. Soon she had two more large piles of cuttings. She lit them and watched the crooked branches reach out from the flames like contorted old arms seeking help. The sight was enough to sadden anyone, but Anna had no time for sorrow. She worked herself into a frenzy trying to be everywhere at once, to cut vines, to light fires, to direct others, to locate more of the insects. By the time Oscar arrived with his own chain saw, early morning light was beginning to find its way over the Valley giving the fighters a better view of their efforts.

Federica also came later in the morning explaining that she hadn't been able to come sooner because she had to get her son off to school.

By midmorning, the group had stacked and burnt all of the vines they suspected of carrying insects.

Anna shook her head at the destruction of so many of their very best Cabernet Sauvignon grape vines. About four acres of the central section was a bleak island lost in the midst of healthy old vines.

"We better spray the rest of these vines just in case." She turned to Oscar for help. "Maybe you would be willing to go into St. Helena for the insecticide? We won't be able to call this field organic for a while, but at least we can avoid a complete loss."

Oscar nodded, understanding her reluctance. Without questioning her, he headed for his truck and town.

The stress of it all suddenly bore down upon Anna.

As though a great weight had fallen upon her, she slumped down to the earth, too emotional to walk away from the vineyard, too tired to even raise herself off the ground.

Federica and Joseph coming up on either side, tried to lift her; but she shrugged off their efforts. She would not allow anyone to raise her from this state of despair, and then slowly began to give in to her misery.

What Anna didn't know was that earlier her sister had sensed just how deeply this loss was hitting Anna so she had called Marco.

Everyone except Anna walked back to the winery. Marco was there when they arrived. "Where is she?" he asked.

"She's out there in the middle of the Emma Mae Vineyard," Federica explained. "She won't speak to anyone or let anyone near her. I thought maybe you could reason with her."

"I'm willing to try, but I haven't been too successful with her in the past."

"I know," Federica said. "But she cares for you more than you know."

Marco nodded his head hoping his ex-sister-in-law's assessment was right. He walked out to the center of the devastated area where Anna sat in an uncommon posture, head down cradled with the palms of her hands. Marco stood quietly near Anna, but soon sat down sharing the ground beside her.

She looked at him almost quizzically and mumbled, "Why did they send you?"

Marco didn't answer. He just handed her a handkerchief.

"I suppose they're all feeling sorry for me now."

"More like concerned about you."

"And you? Why would you care?"

"We once were close."

Anna studied her own feelings toward Marco, and was surprised that more than anyone in her family she was pleased he was the one who was here with her now.

Marco sat quietly, letting her know he would stay as long as necessary.

Finally Anna said, "Aren't you going to help me stand up? I can't sit out here all day."

After she was back on her feet, she began to feel another emotion which she didn't suppress. "Did you see that bastard Donald smile when the police took him away? No, of course, you didn't. You weren't here. What am I thinking anyhow? Am I going mad?"

"You might be getting angry, but, no, you're certainly not going mad."

"That's good to hear."

They walked through the vineyard toward the house. Anna looked at Marco and said softly, "I want you to know that I was surprised yet somehow pleased to see you standing there beside me. I don't know when I've ever felt so low in my life."

"You've lived with these vines for so long, they're so intermingled with you that wine flows with blood through your veins."

"You think I have blood wine?"

"I think you're strong enough to survive."

Marco put an arm around her shoulders and led her out of the vineyard. She didn't resist him, but he was aware she didn't lean toward him either.

When they reached the house, she thanked him with a kiss on the cheek, started to say something, but restrained herself and then went on alone into her bedroom leaving Marco to wonder what course this suspended relationship would take. He certainly couldn't make more clearly his feelings toward her than he just did.

He walked over to the other members of the family who were standing around under the arbor. "I don't know if I helped or not."

"You certainly did, Marco," Federica responded. "You got her out of the field and back in the house where she can relax. Thank you for coming." She gave him a kiss on the cheek, and he reluctantly walked over to his pickup.

CHAPTER 15

While writing out an order for several cases of bottles she needed for the next bottling, Anna's phone began to ring. She had no desire to speak with another salesperson or for that matter with anyone whom she hadn't called. However, the caller did not take a hint and let the unit ring and ring. Finally she lifted the receiver. "Yes. What is it?"

"It's your cousin Donald. I wanted to explain something to you."

"What!!?" Are you out of jail already?"

"I haven't been in jail. All that happened out in the vineyard was a complete misunderstanding. You burned all the evidence anyhow. Lucky me, huh?"

She could almost see the smirk on his face.

"I explained everything to the police. Now if you will just give me a chance—"

"Get off my phone, and don't you ever call me again." She slammed the phone down, almost breaking the cradle with the force of her anger.

Donald didn't call back. He considered writing Anna a letter but knew in her present state she would simply tear it up without reading what he had so say. So he thought he'd try another email. He sent her a message hoping she would read some of it before deleting it completely.

> Dear Anna,
>
> Everything that happened in the vineyard was misunderstood. I had heard that a certain insect was infiltrating local vines, so I thought I would do you a favor by checking without being seen so I wouldn't anger anyone. I was trying to get rid of the ones I discovered because, as you know, I have an interest in the vineyard and wouldn't want anything untoward to happen.
>
> While I was exterminating the pest, that brother-in-law of yours arrived in the dark, misunderstood my movements, and started attacking me.

> I explained all this to the arresting officer and proved that I hold a lien on the place. Plus, I explained how you have chosen to ignore our relationship and have denied me my inheritance. So I was released on my own recognizance.
>
> In this new light, knowing I had intended no harm, I so hope you'll let me make all things right between us. Remember how forthright I was in bringing you a new tractor after someone set fire to the barn? You see, I'm not as bad a person as you might presently believe.
>
> Your Rightful Cousin Who Wants To Make Amends,
> Donald Stanton

Instead of deleting the message, Anna printed it out to show to her father. She remained extremely calm about doing this. In reality she knew now that Donald was not going away any time soon. What she had to do was collect her nerves and deal with him. All sorts of thoughts were passing through her mind. They ranged from hiring someone to get rid of him, or frightening him with threats, or disabling him; but she knew she would not do any of those things. She had to figure out something. It had to be something dramatic, simple, but so effective it would set in his brain forever.

Didn't he say he wanted to meet me sometime someplace? That's perfect! The memory of one of the most upsetting experiences she'd ever suffered came to her just then in her moment of need. Knowing exactly what she would do, she picked up the telephone that was fortunately still working after she had slammed it so hard into its cradle.

She dialed Donald Stanton.

"Yes? Stanton Financial Services. Donald speaking."

"Donald . . ." She paused not quite able to get started explaining her plan.

"Is this Anna?'" he asked, really not sure she would ever call, but to himself he gloated, thinking perhaps he had carried it off.

"Donald, this is hard for me to explain, so hear me out. I read your email, and I don't believe all of your explanation; however, there is a sincerity that I never sensed from you before. I would like to have a good sit-down talk with you."

"Nothing I'd like better," he responded.

"But in order for us to accomplish anything,"Anna explained, "I don't want to meet you here at the winery, or in your place of business either for that matter."

"What do you have in mind?"

"I want to use a neutral territory, preferably not close to Napa or San Francisco."

"Well, where would you like to meet?"

"Some place where our differences could be ironed out. You know what I mean: settled once and for all. Could you get away for a couple of days?"

"I can arrange it."

"Okay. Good. Have you ever been to Mendocino? It's on the northern coast."

"No, but I've heard it's a beautiful place."

"It is. The town is set right above the cliffs facing the ocean, not a big town, easy to find your way around. There are several bed and breakfast places that I've used, but I don't want to make a reservation until we see how the talks go. Could you meet me there two days from now?"

"Yes. I have enough clout to be away whenever I like."

"Okay, two days from today, mark your calendar. Wait at the end of the main street where it curves around on the ocean side. You'll have a great view of the Pacific. I think there might be some benches there. Mendocino is only a few hours' drive, so you should be there about noon if you leave early. Would that be all right by you?"

"Yes. I'm pleased you want to make things right between us."

"Well, we can agree on that for starters."

On the appointed morning, Donald was out of the city before the seven o'clock traffic filled the streets. His black BMW sedan moved him easily at any speed he chose. He headed north on the 101 not slowing until he reached Santa Rosa where he stopped for coffee and a pastry. After that he took the 128 through Yorkville and Boonville and arrived in Mendocino shortly after noon as planned.

He liked the town with its arts and craft businesses lining the main drive and its small-town feel, akin to a New England coastal village. Finding a convenient place to sit, he gazed out over the Pacific contemplating how much he was really enjoying this outing. Should do this sort of thing more often, he thought. After a while he began looking around toward town expecting Anna to arrive any moment and feeling a little tentative about the outcome of their meeting. He would have to say just the right things, and handle her carefully. She was tough, he knew; but then she asked for this opportunity, so he wanted to be sure to make the most out of it.

* * *

At the same time Donald was sitting on the edge of the continent in a waiting mode, Anna was going into one of the wine tunnels built to sustain a constant temperature. The coolness of the air and the scent of aging wines bolstered by the nearness of the dome-shaped sculpted, gray stone walls, all combined to ease her away from the stress her would-be cousin had inflicted on her.

She had no intention of ever meeting Stanton in Mendocino or any other place. The memory that had prompted this course of action was one she had experienced while in her teens. Marco had promised to meet her on the front steps of the school. When he didn't show, she realized how much she cared for the handsome schoolmate. He didn't come around, but she was very stubborn. The longer she waited, the more miserable she felt. She began to fear he was toying with her emotions. Nevertheless, she stayed on for the worst two hours of her life. At first she felt anger, but then a growing sense of emptiness and betrayal.

The principal of the school had walked by and saw her sitting on the concrete steps. "Anna, what are doing here?"

"I'm waiting for Marco, but I guess he just doesn't care about me."

"Haven't you heard?"

"No. What?"

"Marco is in the hospital. He broke his arm in football practice. I'm going to visit him right now. You are welcome to come along with me if you like."

"No, thanks. He probably didn't want to see me anyway. I think I'll just walk home."

"I'll tell him you were waiting for him."

"He won't care. He could have let me know somehow."

As Anna walked dejectedly away, the man shook his head. Even though he worked with teenagers every day, he wouldn't claim for a moment he understood everything there was to know about them.

As Anna recalled that painful memory, she left the coolness of the tunnel and went back into her office. Waiting in vain hurts: I know from experience. Well, Stanton can wait for an eternity. He will never see me coming to him. I hope he falls into a pit of despair. She switched off her cell phone, and then set her computer to block all email originating from Donald Stanton.

The office phone rang before she could tell her father not to answer it. When he heard Stanton's voice and saw Anna vigorously shaking her head from side to side and tapping her finger on her lips gesturing not to speak, he instantly realized something was happening. He held the phone to his ear for a while without responding and then placed the headset in the cradle cutting off Donald's monologue in mid-sentence.

"That was Stanton. What's going on?"

"Something I arranged. I hope he is suffering."

"He sounded distraught, but I couldn't figure what the call was all about."

"I want him to suffer. I want him to realize any attempt to become part of our family will get him nowhere."

"What did you do?

"I sent him up to Mendocino letting him believe I would meet him there. Now he can stay until a tsunami comes on or a high tide drowns him for all I care."

"So he's waiting up there hoping to see you?"

"Right! I know how it feels to wait for someone who never shows. I want to force him to realize how much he has hurt us and what a ridiculous person this compulsion has made him become."

Anna stood up and deliberately walked out of the office, but she paused for a moment and turned to her father. "Dad, come along with me. Will you?"

Surprised at her request, he could only agree. She led him into the tunnel that contained the new barrels with the aging Emma Mae Vineyard wines. She drew out a portion with a wine thief, then poured a little in two glasses. She swirled it, sniffed it, and drank a couple of sips, then motioned for her father to do the same.

"You want my opinion on this?"

"Yes. This is important. The wine in these barrels could be the best we've ever had. The secondary fermentation was completed before barreling. It's completely stable, very good specific gravity. I still want you to check it out. I can't take the chance of producing another disaster."

Joseph nodded, and before swirling the liquid, he studied it for clarity. Without comment he sniffed, then tasted, and finally said, "This wine is clear, velvety soft, beginning to develop body, and already sends off a wonderful aroma. I have to say that your new barrels have given this a fine complexity. I believe it's the best Cabernet at this early age I've ever tasted."

"I agree," Anna said smiling. "Do you believe it's ready for bottling?"

"Anna, you're the vintner. I don't want to wander into your territory."

"You won't be. I'm asking for your advice, but I'll make the final decision."

Joseph was certain about the wine; however, he didn't want to upset their relationship which had so improved lately. With caution he said, "It hasn't been in the oak very long. That's good because new oak transfers flavor quickly. I suppose just a little more time in the barrel would be enough and then you should bottle it, but only if you plan to let it age in the bottle for a couple of years."

"Thank you, Dad. That's exactly what I thought. I feel good about this. It's time we got things right around here."

"Now that we've accomplished making this decision, there is one thing I do want to ask you."

"Ask away. You won't upset me."

"Okay. Here goes: are you planning to use those plastic or synthetic corks you once talked about?"

"No, I'm not. The corks you've been buying are delivered clean, as bacteria-free and good as anything available. We have a new supply and the glass Freddie ordered will be here soon. Scott has shown Steve how to keep our vintage bottler working properly so we're in good shape."

She paused thinking maybe a little more explanation would help matters. "Dad, I'll stay with tradition until something proves itself to be better." She nodded her head, agreeing with herself and explained,

"I learned a valuable lesson from my wild fermentation experiment with that natural mold."

* * *

Donald Stanton did not get sullen, or depressed, or feel abandoned. He'd been alone all his life. Waiting for someone who didn't show up meant nothing because he hadn't really cared for anyone in particular. In reality, Anna seemed no more of a relative to him than any stranger who walked by on the street.

When he finally realized she was not coming and wouldn't answer his calls, he did not go into a period of self-evaluation as Anna had hoped. He went through several stages from surprise that he could be so easily duped, then resentment, followed by anger that he was so poorly treated, and finally bitter renunciation of Anna and her father. They were denying him the inheritance he had worked for, sacrificed, trained, planned, and was convinced, he deserved.

With his anger bordering on madness, he drove recklessly back to his San Francisco apartment, slept fitfully, made an irrevocable decision and arose determined to remove all barriers from his supposed entitlement.

Since he had taken time off from work, he figured he might as well use the time to prepare for his final solution. In the morning, after waiting for traffic to lighten, he drove over the Bay Bridge to Oakland. Parking in a lot just off Jack London Square, he watched cargo being off-loaded, and wondered just where a foreigner coming to California might look if he wanted to secure papers which would allow him to remain in the States. Actually that was not quite what he needed. He left the Square and strolled around until he found an area with used-clothing shops, a scabby diner and several pawnshops. He didn't see what he wanted in any window display, so he entered the seediest pawnshop on the block.

A slovenly-looking man, bald on top with scraggly hair around the sides of his head and stringy strands hanging down the back, stood behind a barred window.

"Lookin' for a tattoo?" the operator asked.

"Strange thing to ask about in a pawnshop," Donald said.

"You don't look like my usual customer either. So what is it you want?"

"Would you have any kind of handgun? For protection, of course," he added.

"Unmarked, no doubt?"

"That wouldn't matter."

"It would to me," the man scoffed. "You look too inexperienced to be a cop. So why do you need a piece?"

"Protection, I told you."

The guy went into a back room and eventually came out with two tarnished semi-automatic pistols. "There's no known history on these," he smirked. "They'll cost you."

"Kind of old. Do they work?"

The man held up the larger one and pulled the slide back into the cocked position and pulled the trigger.

The loud metallic click startled Donald.

"You don't know much about guns, do you?"

"I can handle one. I know that's a Police 45. I wonder how you got it."

He didn't respond to the remark, but said, "Seven fifty for both of them."

"I only want one. How much for the smaller one, the .32 caliber?"

"Four hundred, cash."

"Can you throw in a silencer?"

"You are serious, aren't you?"

"Never mind the small talk. Yes or no?"

"Three hundred for a good silencer." Donald looked skeptical so the man added, "I'll throw in a box of shells so you won't have to register any of these purchases. That suit you?"

"Yeah, fine." Donald counted out seven one-hundred-dollar bills while the shop owner wiped the gun and silencer clean of his own prints.

He placed the items in a small dark canvas bag. "Anything else?"

"I do have a question." The man stared blankly at Stanton without interest. Stanton finally said, "Anyone around here who can make up a new driver's license? I lost mine and can't even rent a car."

"Yeah, sure." The guy almost laughed out loud. "I don't know of anyone around here, but you'll find people like that over near the Embarcadero."

"Got an address?"

"I might."

"Okay. How much will that info cost me?"

"I'll let you off easy, just fifty. You're such a good customer."

Donald counted out another fifty dollars while the man scratched out the address from memory. He took the canvas bag and headed back to his car.

* * *

On the morning the Emma Mae bottling was to begin, Scott and Federica got their son off to school. Sandy refused a ride because he liked the freedom of riding his bike so after school he could choose when and where he would go. He figured his parents would be home late. They were always late when the time for bottling came around.

His mother must have read his mind. "You can ride your bike, but I'll be back here waiting for you before school lets out. Don't be late!"

"Okay. I know the rules." He sighed and nodded his head.

Federica called her assistant Leticia asking if she would like to experience the important stage of moving wine this time from barrel to bottle. The girl agreed at once. "I'll ride in with my Dad this morning. He's getting ready to leave."

Anna hadn't heard from Donald Stanton in over three weeks. No emails, no calls, no communication of any sort. She was so hoping that having put some distance between them would give the creep a lasting idea of what she thought about him. As each quiet day passed, she relaxed a bit more.

Joseph and Anna were already setting up the equipment when the others arrived. Anna greeted her sister, but with more joy than she had shown her in a long time. She was especially happy Scott came along because Steve had to help his father with an important order. She hugged Scott and planted a strong kiss on his cheek. "So glad you're here, Scott. If you can keep this temperamental bottling machine running for the next couple of days, I'll be forever grateful."

"I'll show it who's boss."

Oscar set to unwrapping the corks and setting them in place. Scott checked to be sure the corker aligned correctly with the bottles. Federica brought Leticia with her to the tunnels so they could unfurl the hoses and set them up to siphon the wine from barrel to glass. It was also their job to continue setting the empty bottles on the line. Joseph and Anna worked at the end of the conveyor belt gathering the filled bottles and carrying them back to the tunnels to give the wine a rest. They were stacking the wine horizontally in racks where they would be left for time to work its subtle changes on the vintage.

Anna felt very good about getting the Emma Mae Cab into bottles. As she was carrying an armload, she said to her father, "Everything would be perfect if we had enough of the new labels with our *Dancing Horse* logo. We used the few new ones we had on wines that went to France for Marco's order."

"Well," he spoke without much enthusiasm, "we can always order more and apply them later."

"What's wrong, Dad? You don't seem happy. This is a great day."

"I'm worried."

"Our analysis showed the pH level was excellent. We don't even need to blend with a higher or lower acidity. All indications are this will be one of the finest wines we've ever made. Are you concerned because I have handled all phases of this from the beginning?"

"No. Certainly not."

"What is it then?"

Joseph shook his head slowly with great concern. "I just can't believe Stanton will stay away from here."

"Perhaps he finally caught on. If we're lucky, maybe he will go on to live his own life—somewhere else, back in L.A. preferably."

"For everyone's sake, I hope so."

About then, Marco arrived unannounced, dressed in jeans and a work shirt. "Can you use any more help here?"

"All we can get." Anna was pleased to be able to get on to another subject. She let Marco give her a little hug, kissed him lightly on the lips and asked him to help Freddie and Leticia who had more than they could handle with siphoning, filling, and restocking the bottles.

Federica and Leticia noticed the quick kiss and exchanged a smile.

"That reminds me," Federica said to Leticia. "Anything going on between you and that handsome young man, Steve Stavos?"

"The cooper's son? No. He's a little old for me, don't you think? We're just friends."

"Well, that's the way things get started."

"Let's get back to work," Leticia suggested.

CHAPTER 16

Donald Stanton had driven by the winery looking for an opportunity to carry out his plan. As he passed by in the late afternoon, he saw a number of cars and pickup trucks parked in the driveway and out front along the highway. The only thing he knew for certain was that whatever was going on at the winery didn't involve him, so with seething resentment he drove on. Driving by again late the next afternoon, he saw that a dinner was being held under the grape arbor by the stone building. He observed people interacting, laughing, and raising glasses for some kind of celebration. None of that included him for now, but he knew that would change when he became the sole owner of the winery. Maybe on his next visit there wouldn't be so much going on with all those people around so perhaps he would have a chance to set his plan in action.

His vacation days were over so he returned to work. However, the time off had done nothing to alter his design. Stanton felt so manipulated by his experience in Mendocino that he now harbored a hatred that was eating away at his core. He could not readily get his mind back to the bank's finances. Sitting alone in his glass-walled office, he mentally went through his final preparations. He knew he had to move precisely without mistakes.

* * *

Joseph and Anna had returned to their wine cellar where they worked together checking the bottles for clarity and then placing them on their side in the racks for bottle aging.

"It'll be two years before we see any return on this wine, but I believe we have an outstanding vintage," Anna said to her father. "Thank you for having trust in me."

"Always have. Those arguments we had are part of the process."

Later in the evening, Joseph was tired but deeply satisfied with the bottling they had finished and with Anna's development into a good vintner. He went to bed and was soon snoring lightly.

Anna was in her room preparing for bed. Just before she fell asleep, she smiled remembering Marco's comment that she would like to be

Wine Goddess of the Valley. Not really, she thought, but the image struck her as funny. She soon fell asleep dreaming within a dream that her desire to become a successful vintner was coming true.

A few hundred yards from the vineyard entrance a dark gray nondescript sedan pulled off the road. Donald Stanton, dressed totally in black, pulled a ski mask down over his face and stepped out of the car. His eyes stared through the circular openings with unblinking intensity.

He walked on silent sneakers to the Pugliesi's home. Using a master key designed for older doors, he unlocked the front door and cautiously entered the living room. Hearing Joseph's snoring let him know where to go first.

Enough light filtered in through a window so that he could see his target lying on the bed. Without hesitating, he pointed the pistol at Joseph and fired twice at the body.

Two muffled sounds issued from the gun, followed by a quick jerk and a groan from Joseph. Stanton waited for any more sounds or movement from the elder Pugliesi. Satisfied that he didn't have to shoot again, he moved away going through the living room and kitchen, heading for Anna's bedroom in the rear of the house.

As he entered her room, he heard the click of the outside door being unlocked. Marco entered from outside.

"What the hell?" Marco yelled when he saw the figure in black.

Anna bolted upright as Stanton fired at her. The bullet pulverized the pillow where her head had been a moment before.

Marco leaped across the room ramming Stanton against the wall with all the force he could muster. Another shot went wild up into the ceiling. Anna rushed over and tried to wrestle the gun away from Stanton. When Stanton attempted to push her away, Marco struck him with a solid blow to the side of his head with a fist. He staggered backward and Marco pulled the ski mask off.

For a few moments Stanton stood dazed, but quickly recovered and tried again to fight off Marco. He was no match for Marco who grabbed him, twisted him around, and shoved him down on his face. He then dug both knees into his back and yanked his arms behind him.

Anna used a thin leather belt to wrap around Stanton's wrists and then tied them into a secure knot she knew would not be easy to loosen.

She said to Marco, "He came through the house. I wonder if he was in Dad's room! You'd think my father would have heard all the noise in here!"

She ran into his bedroom, saw her father lying motionless, and did a quick check for breath and pulse. She determined he was alive but unconscious.

"Hold that bastard!" she yelled out to Marco and then wasted no time dialing 911 asking for an ambulance and police. When she told the operator her father had been shot and where she was calling from, the woman knew the winery location. The dispatch was instant.

The fire rescue unit arrived first. The woman attempted to stop the bleeding, but could only apply pressure points around Joseph's shoulder and hip. With the help of the local police who had also arrived, they carefully placed Joseph on a gurney and carried him to the emergency vehicle. The rescue workers gave him oxygen and rushed him to St. Helena Hospital.

The officers first questioned Anna and Marco, then quickly read a strangely subdued Donald Stanton his rights before snapping on handcuffs and taking him into custody.

As soon as the officers left, Marco said, "C'mon, Anna, let me take you to the hospital."

"I can drive."

"I know you can, but I'd rather be with you."

She saw a concerned look in his eyes she'd never understood before. "Let's not lose any time."

On the drive to the hospital, Anna let him know her feelings: "You're a wonderful man, Marco. Seems lately, you're always there when I need you. You saved my life in the bedroom tonight, you know?"

He squeezed her hand but kept his attention on the driving.

Marco found a parking space near the emergency room. The ER nurse told them she had rushed Joseph through the triage. "His vital signs are weak, but he's alive. He is already in surgery."

"Can we see him?"

"Of course you can, but not for a while."

"He looked bad, didn't he?"

"We have fine doctors here, the best," the nurse assured Anna. "You may use the waiting room, but before you leave there are some forms you need to fill out."

"Why don't you take care of the forms?" Marco suggested. "I'll try to find one of the doctors who can tell us about your father's condition."

Anna hurriedly filled out the forms with as much information as she could and went in search of Marco.

He was in the waiting room when Anna arrived. "No one knows any more about Joseph than the two doctors who are operating. We'll just have to wait to talk with them."

They sat for a full two hours before a doctor came in.

"How is he?"

"Your father is a strong man, miss. One bullet went in below the right shoulder, grazed the clavicle, and did some damage to the muscle. The more serious damage was done to the left hip. We removed the bullet and did what we could for now. The joint has been shattered."

"Will he be able to walk?"

The doctor answered, "It's much too early to tell. We have controlled the blood flow and are just keeping him stable for now."

"He's going to live. He'll be all right, won't he?"

"I believe so. The hip will need repair, perhaps a replacement. His ability to walk will be determined later. If all goes right, the shoulder should return to its normal function."

"Is he awake?" Marco asked.

"He was, but he's sedated. You may look in on him. Don't try to wake him. He's been in shock, but he has come out of it and is now sleeping."

Anna had never before seen her father in a hospital bed. She had always considered him a permanent presence which for personal reasons she often railed against. Lying there, wrapped in tape, barely breathing, tubes issuing from his damaged body, he seemed to her so unreal.

She glanced at Marco. "The doctor said his hip needs repair. If he means a hip replacement, why didn't they do it when he was in surgery?"

"It's not that simple, Anna. First of all, he has to get over the shock of being hit with two bullets. A human body can take only so much punishment."

"I'm sure you're right. Dad was always able to defend himself. Right now he seems so vulnerable."

"Well, now he has you to take care of him."

"I will, but now I won't be able to find anything to complain about."

Marco shook his head sympathetically with her attempt at humor regarding such a serious matter. "C'mon, Anna, we should let him rest. Let's go."

Marco drove Anna home. When he walked her to the house, she said, "Marco, don't take this wrong, but will you spend the night here with me?"

"What could be wrong with that?" he said and then withdrew the question. "Of course, I'll stay. I wouldn't think you'd want to be alone tonight."

"I want you to stay, but I didn't want you to think it might be a permanent arrangement."

"Anna, I'll never force myself on you. Tonight, I think you need some rest."

* * *

In the morning, while they were having coffee, a loud knock came at the front door. Marco went to find out who was knocking.

A well-dressed, middle-aged Latino man introduced himself, "Good morning, I'm Investigator Jesus Morales with the St. Helena Police Department."

"I suppose you want to speak with Anna?"

"Yes, but if you're Marco, I wish to speak with you also."

"Come in," Anna said, stepping up to the door. "We're just having coffee. Care for some?"

"Actually, I would very much like a cup."

Anna poured him a cup of coffee, but before saying anything further she waited to see how he would approach his investigation.

Jesus spoke softly with a good degree of confidence. He sat at the kitchen table and slowly stirred the coffee. "I read the officer's report this morning. What I'd mostly like to do right now is check out the places where the shooting occurred. I understand one hit your pillow and another went into the ceiling in your bedroom."

"Yes, and two hit my father."

"I know," Jesus explained. "I called the hospital this morning. Your father is resting. I suppose you'll be going to visit him soon?"

"Of course."

"If you will first show me the places where the shooting happened, I'll try not to take too much of your time. Later today I would like both of you to stop by the station."

Marco, tried to save Anna from further distress by saying: "We already spoke with the two officers who were here last night. They also took the gun as evidence."

"I know, but this is my investigation now. I need a statement from both of you. I want everything to proceed by the book so there will no question about improprieties."

"I understand," Anna said. "I fully agree with you. We'll come by your office when we leave the hospital. Will that be okay?"

Jesus took photos of the pillow, the hole in the ceiling, and Joseph's bed where blood had stained the sheets. He carefully wrote his observations and then sat down to finish the second cup of coffee Anna offered him.

* * *

Joseph was awake when Anna and Marco walked into his hospital room. There was an IV in his left arm, a bandage wrapped around his right shoulder, and more wrapping on the left hip. He was still groggy and speaking slowly.

"Are you in a lot of pain, Dad?"

"No, honey, they pumped me full of pain medicine. I feel kind of light-headed like I'm floating somewhere off in space."

Marco was really shocked by how weak Joseph looked, but he tried to say something positive. "You look a lot better than you did last night when they took you away."

"I don't know what happened. They said someone shot me."

"Yes," Anna explained, "Donald Stanton broke in while we were sleeping. He tried to shoot me, too, but Marco came by just in time to stop him."

"Did you get him?"

"Yes, he was arrested."

"That's a relief." Joseph sighed and sagged back into the bed. "Marco, I have to thank you. I think you know how much Anna means to me."

"Yes, sir. She means a great deal to me, too."

"Dad, if Marco stayed with us for a while, would that be all right by you?"

Marco certainly heard what she had said but didn't respond at the time.

"That's a good idea. You shouldn't be alone right now anyhow," Joseph agreed.

"The doctor told us you might need a hip replacement. We need your consent. When the time comes, will that be all right by you?"

"I guess I don't have much of a choice. One of them looked in on me early this morning. He said they would be taking X-rays today, and he would know more after that. I guess they cleaned up a lot of bone fragments; however, there was serious damage."

"Oh, Dad, I'm sorry you have to go through this. Maybe I shouldn't have sent that monster out on a wild goose chase, but I had to do something to get him out of our life." She couldn't hold back the weeping which rose up into her eyes.

Marco drew her close and held her.

"Don't blame yourself, Anna," Joseph said. "No one could have predicted. I'll be all right." He sighed and lay back into the bed. "I think I better rest now. Marco, I know you'll take good care of her for me."

"Of course I will." Marco placed a hand on Joseph's good shoulder in complete agreement with his concerns, then led Anna out of the room and to his pickup.

They drove directly to the police station. In his office, Jesus Morales greeted Anna and Marco as though they were long-time friends. He had taken off his jacket and loosened his tie. He spoke with an understanding of their distress: "I hope you won't mind if I tape our conversation."

Anna said, "I don't mind, but before we start I want to ask you something."

"Go ahead."

"Where is Donald Stanton now and what will be happening to him?"

"As of now, he's in custody without bail. When we finish our investigation, he will be turned over to the Napa Country district attorney, who, I might add, is a tough one."

Marco had remained quiet but couldn't help asking, "Will he be charged with attempted manslaughter?"

"Before I can answer that, let's get on with the investigation. I want to speak with each of you separately. Who would like to be first?"

"I will," Anna said wanting to get this matter over with.

"Marco, if you will leave us for a while. You'll find coffee in the waiting room."

Jesus turned on the recorder and handled the interviews with concerned professionalism. When finished, he walked the couple to the door, shook hands, and thanked them for being cooperative.

They left feeling there was a good chance justice might be served. On the ride home, Marco observed, "Jesus Morales was very impressive, really had his act together. A man like him could work his way up to becoming chief of police."

"You know, Marco, you always see people through rose-colored glasses. He's a nice guy, but I doubt if he's tough enough to become police chief."

Marco frowned because he realized that even though he and Anna were closer than they had been in a long time, there would always be that friction between them. "Anna, I hope you're not going to counter everything I say."

"Why would you expect me to be any different?"

"Now that we have gotten together, I thought perhaps you might want it to last."

"Always the optimist, aren't you, Marco?"

"Even to the point of thinking we might make it work this time."

They rode quietly until they were nearly home, and Anna said, "I've been thinking about that area in the Emma Mae Vineyard. You know the section we had to burn to get rid of the insects?"

"Yes, about two or three acres, wasn't it?"

She nodded. "More like four. I'm thinking of expanding that and planting something special there."

Marco released a breath of air from the relief knowing they wouldn't be starting another dispute so soon. "Want to let me know what it is? I'd like to help you with it if possible," he offered. "I know places where good bud root is available. We can buy all we need."

"Dad used to make a few bottles of Sangiovese from his father-in-law's vineyards in Sonoma. As I remember, it wasn't bad. In fact, it was one of the best wines he ever developed."

"I can get that."

"No, I don't want to plant Sangiovese. I'm just saying that Dad made a very good wine with that grape. I have something else in mind."

"I guess you're not going to tell me."

"Not right now. I have to do more research."

"But it is something you have been wanting to try?"

"Yes, but let's hold on. I also want to tell my father about this plan. It will give him something to look forward to."

* * *

Marco drove Anna to the hospital the next day. They walked directly to Joseph's room with the proposed plan. But Joseph was not able to receive good news. In fact he wasn't in his room. The attending nurse told them he was back in intensive care.

When Anna found the physician, she was told her father had suffered a stroke during the night and that he was currently being attended to.

"How could that have happened?" she asked the man.

"A blood clot formed during the night and prevented flow to his brain."

"Can't that be removed?"

"We're treating him. He's still unconscious. We don't know as of now how much damage has occurred."

"This is terrible. How could you let this happen?"

"The trauma of two bullets is always severe."

"Was it because of all the damage done to his hip?"

"More likely it was the result of torn arteries when the bullet went through his shoulder and traveled upward. We found a clot had moved and entered the brainstem, stopping the flow of blood to his brain."

"Have you taken it out?"

"No. We have given him blood thinners. It's extremely dangerous to remove. If it is moved to either side, it would be fatal."

"This is the worst kind of news. What can be done?"

"We have contacted a neurosurgeon from San Francisco General, the very best in his field. He can be here in a matter of hours. We have to ask for your permission concerning a possible procedure."

"What are his chances?"

"We would rather you spoke with the surgeon after he conducts his examination."

"Why are you waiting? Have him fly here immediately."

"I'll place the call," the doctor answered.

Anna asked, "May I see my father?"

"I would advise against it. You wouldn't be able to speak with him. He is medicated and on life support. Excuse me. I must leave now to call the surgeon and to prepare for possible surgery." He walked hurriedly away.

"This is terrible!" Anna went into the waiting room and collapsed into a chair.

Marco tried to console her. After a while he said, "Would you like to have your sister here with you? I can call her for you."

"No, let me do it. She should hear the news from me." Anna used her cell phone to call Federica at the winery and gave her the updated report.

"Oh no! That's terrible. I'll be right there." She asked her two aides, Leticia and Steve, to take over. She dropped what she was doing and rushed out to her car.

When Federica walked in the waiting room, Anna went to her immediately. She hugged her sister for a long time without saying anything.

"How is he, Anna?"

Through tears, she managed to answer, "It's very bad. Each report gets worse."

"He's not going to die, is he?"

"No one knows. There's a specialist coming in from San Francisco. He will be here as soon as possible." Anna returned to the couch she'd been sitting on, dropped her head in her hands and sighed.

Federica looked at her sister, quite surprised at how hard she was taking this news. She sat beside Anna, putting an arm around her shoulders.

"I shouldn't have been so harsh with him," Anna admitted. "I was a real bitch."

"You always said what you thought, but you two have been getting along very well lately."

"It may be too late," Anna said.

After a half hour, Federica rose slowly. "Stay with her, will you, Marco? I'm going to find someone who knows what's going on with our father."

Marco took the seat beside Anna. She leaned against him accepting his affection. In a while they heard a helicopter approaching the hospital, and then waited for what seemed an interminable amount of time until Federica finally appeared.

Walking very slowly, Federica paused and then spoke with the calmest voice she could find, "I saw the doctor arriving and waited until he had a chance to examine Dad." She choked up unable to continue.

"What's wrong? What did he say?"

"He's gone, Anna. Dad had a second stroke. It was too late for anyone to do anything."

CHAPTER 17

Marco waited in the limo while Federica went into the house to get Anna for the funeral. "We have the car ready for you."

Anna sat at the kitchen table. She drank a cup of coffee but couldn't eat anything. "I'm not ready for this. Dad wasn't ready either."

"I know," Federica said. "He was far too young. It's terribly hard to take."

"Why didn't that stupid Donald Stanton just come to visit us like a normal person? He could have explained that Joseph was his father's half brother. We had some knowledge of the circumstances so we wouldn't have been too shocked to learn Dad was born out of wedlock. So our grandmother chose to name him Pugliesi. So what? His father never came back to visit or tried to help raise him. Two generations later some guy shows up claiming he should own the winery. Without letting us know who he is, he takes the low road, the dark side, and strives to manipulate his way into the family.

"I feel it's also a very personal matter. How could he try to stop me from my destiny? I was born into this life. It is all I know and all I ever wanted to do. Something eternal happens on this parcel of earth. I have to do my part to keep it alive."

After attending the services and the burial, Anna wanted nothing more than to be alone. She dismissed Federica and her assistants, and wouldn't let Marco stay with her. She had to think things through until she figured how to accept this turn of events.

The loss of her father had disturbed Anna far more personally than she had expected. Though she felt she loved him, she always considered him an obstruction she had to work around. Now there was something so enormous missing from her life, an immense unfilled chasm. She couldn't fathom how she could ever have believed she could do without him or that she would be better off running the winery without his patient guidance and experienced advice, and the love he gave without asking for anything in return.

The man was always there, had always been there. She had felt that his presence quietly dominated her. Yet that was not the case, not the kind of person he really was. She was a fool and should've known better, should have appreciated what she had when she'd had it.

* * *

Three weeks after the services, Federica got a call from a prison inmate. Curious, she accepted the call.

"Federica, I always thought of you as the kindest of the Pugliesi family."

"Who is this?"

A hesitant voice said, "Donald Stanton."

"Stanton! I thought you were out of our lives forever."

"I wanted to contact you to explain how much I regret what happened. I know I'm in deeper trouble than ever."

"I don't care to hear anything from you."

"Will you at least tell Anna I'm sorry for what I did? I'm not denying anything. I'd really like it if she could give me a call sometime."

"Ridiculous! If I know her, she would probably tell you to wait for hell to freeze over before she'd call you."

She hung up and immediately called Anna to tell her about the phone call. Anna's first reaction was to have prison calls blocked from her cell phone, her office phone, and her home phone.

Two days later she received a call on her office phone. It was Donald Stanton.

"How did you get through? I blocked all calls from you."

"I borrowed a private cell phone. Please, don't hang up. There's something you must know."

"I only want to know why you are not going to the gas chamber."

"At my hearing, I admitted to everything. I accepted full responsibility so the judge was lenient. I am deeply sorry for the suffering I caused. I can't expect you to forgive me, but I have nowhere else to turn. I have no other family and no real friends. I know I self-destructed. I am totally to blame."

Anna responded with silence, so Donald continued, "I carried out those actions not knowing what I was doing. I must have been detached from my real self. I was out of my mind. I'm not claiming insanity, exactly. I don't know what came over me except that I made a shambles of my life. You must know I deeply regret all my behavior and that I am grieving over your loss. I only accomplished making a complete disaster of my life and seriously damaged yours.

"I was hoping that some time in the future you might find it within you, if not to forgive me, but perhaps to give me a call as you would to any other relative in trouble."

Only silence from Anna.

Apparently he couldn't feel the searing hate emanating through the phone so he continued talking, "Eventually there will come a day when I will I have a parole hearing, and it would be good at a time like that to have maintained contact with someone who understands."

"So that's why you are calling. You want me to save your ass. Well, let's be clear on this: the day you bring my father back to life is the day I will call you."

She slammed the phone down in the receiver and let out a blast of constrained air.

* * *

The next morning she lay in bed recalling the terrible phone call and also remembering the good things about her father. She wondered if maybe she had never really let herself know the wonderful man and understanding father he had been.

That morning, through her bedroom window, Anna looked away from her thoughts. She could see the first signs of spring. Leaves on the ivy growing along the sides of the stone winery were showing their greening nature. To her right, she had a good view of the Emma Mae Vineyard with rows of yellow mustard poking up in scattered patches beneath the barren branches. She also saw the central section where the rows of vines were missing because they had been sheared off and burnt to protect the rest of the field from the glassy-winged sharpshooter. Surprising to her, Mario, Scott, Steve, and Leticia were out there in the vineyard doing something to the remaining rootstock.

Were they digging out the roots? What was going on? she wondered. I didn't give instructions for anyone to tamper with that section. She pulled on a pair of jeans and a shirt. When she got of the door, she saw Federica drive up to the winery with Scott's pickup. The box was loaded higher than the cab with vine cuttings.

"What's going on here?" Anna asked.

"Oh," Federica explained, "it's a conspiracy to pull you out of your despair."

"Does it really show that much?"

"C'mon, you don't think we know how you feel? And Marco! He's really worried about you. He says you won't see him, you won't talk with him."

"So he's out there digging up the Emma Mae Vineyard to make me feel better, or maybe to make me angry?"

"No, he's doing neither of the above. They are all out there preparing the vine roots for these cuttings. We know you've been wanting to make a good Pinot Noir. This is our surprise."

"Hold on now. You will just have to take them all back."

"Aren't you pleased? Marco knew where to get these prime cuttings."

"He should have checked with me."

"You haven't exactly been available for a long time."

"Then he should have known better. Pinot Noir grapes need limestone soil. I had the land assayed. It is not suitable for Pinot Noir."

"Well, did you tell anyone, especially Marco?"

"No, I didn't. I figured it was my concern."

"Marco is the first one you should've told," Federica explained. "He's been doing everything he can think of to bring you around, and you won't confide in him or even see him. You're such a hard-headed fool. No wonder you can't keep a marriage or even hold a good relationship."

Anna was surprised at Federica's boldness, but she stood her ground and took her sister's remarks.

"You might have discussed with someone else what you were planning to do. You think you have all the answers and don't need anyone else. Look what happened with Donald Stanton. You told no one about that either. Your ridiculous scheme backfired, and we lost our father as a result."

That comment really hit Anna where it hurt. She didn't try to retaliate.

Federica stormed off to tell the others to drop what they're doing and leave the Wine Goddess alone to do her brooding.

While the group was returning from the vineyard, Anna did a bit of thinking, almost to the point of questioning herself.

When they arrived, she was the first to speak, "I appreciate what you were trying to do out there in the vineyard. I'm sorry you went to all this trouble to make me feel better. I guess I should have been more open with my thoughts."

Federica was still uptight. "You're darn right you should have, instead of moping around feeling sorry for yourself. You think no one else cares about what happened?"

"You must know how bad I feel about the loss we've all suffered."

"Then you don't have to carry it alone."

"You're right, Freddie."

A heavy silence set in until Marco spoke up, "Anna, what is it you have in mind for the Emma Mae Vineyard? None of us want more friction."

"I want to thank all of you for being so considerate. I'm to blame for not letting you know my choice of vines. I want to make an exceptional wine from the soil of that vineyard. I wasn't brooding all the time. I've ordered budwood from Burgundy in France and Tuscany in Central Italy. My plan is to grow grapes from vines of both areas and blend these into a velvety, satiny-smooth wine. This time I plan to inoculate with a yeast proven from the Pasteur Institute.

"We all know California wines reached a notable level when it triumphed over the French in the 1976 tasting. Now I believe we're ready for another breakthrough. More people are including wine with their dinners and associate wine with good friends, good times, with celebrations of success or milestones achieved. Since we are located between Calistoga in the warm north and the cool Carneros in the south, we're between Region II and III, actually closer to the north and at the foot of the Mayacamas where the volcanic soil is rich for growing many grape varieties. So what I'm trying to say is that we have the right micro-climate here and the fertile soil to make a wine that will surpass the best Grand Cru or Premier Cru made anywhere."

"And what is this grape you are importing?" Marco asked.

"It's already grown in several places around California, but I wanted to go back in time as close as I could get to the source. I'm sending for vines from the original planting in Europe, to outdo anything we have on this continent."

"What is the wine?" Marco almost pleaded.

"The grape is the elegant Nebbiolo, and we'll grow it with some of the acreage from the Emma Mae Vineyard."

"Ahh, now I understand."

"Do you think it's possible?"

"Yes," he said with some reservation in his tone.

Anna addressed her sister, "Freddie, will you return those cuttings? If they won't refund your money, I'll make it up to you."

"No problem. I'll take care of it."

"Did I ever tell you how much I appreciate you?"

"I don't recall hearing anything quite like that. On one occasion you said I was a good cellar master."

"Exactly, well, you are, and I do treasure you." Anna hugged her sister as she never had before. She was just about to give a little attention to Marco when she noticed a sudden change in the weather.

A counterclockwise low pressure drifted in from north to south bringing cold arctic air down the Valley.

"Good thing we were not planting today," Marco said as the wind whipped up dust clouds.

Scott tied a tarp over the pickup truck box to prevent the contents from blowing away. Gusts of wind fifty to sixty miles per hour scratched across the Valley floor swirling light debris into the air. Everyone rushed into the winery to escape the dust and small flying objects.

Anna poured a glass of her father's White Zinfandel for everyone. "The first drink is to honor the man who made this."

Everyone drank, even Leticia took a few sips.

"My mom says it's okay to taste wine if I'm going to earn a living making it."

"She's right," Steve added. "Those Greeks I met never had any problems and had been introduced to it since they were young."

In about twenty minutes, the wind let up but the air remained extremely cold. Federica said, "We better get home to see if Sandy is all right."

"Why wouldn't he be?" Scott asked but, of course, went outside right away to take Federica home.

"I don't think my dad will be coming by," Leticia said. "Steve, will you give me a ride home?"

"Of course," he agreed, more than willing. As they left he wanted to hold her hand more than anything, but Leticia kept both hands firmly in her pockets. Feeling the cold outside, Steve wrapped his coat over her shoulders.

Anna saw the action and shook her head. "Poor Steve is really taken with that girl. She is so determined to complete her education, he'll have to wait a long time for her."

"Not as long as I've had to wait."

A strange look came over her face. She squinted her eyes as though she was looking inward.

Marco couldn't help noticing the expression. "Anything wrong?"

"No," she said thoughtfully.

"Let's go out to check on the vines," he suggested. "See if there's been any wind damage."

"No, not yet. There's something I want to say to you. I better get it out while I can." She hesitated, not able to put into words what she intended.

He felt a chill wondering if this would be their breakup point. "It must be important," he said trying to get her to release her thoughts, good or bad.

"It's very important. Right now I don't feel I'm a very good person. Freddie blames me for what Stanton did. I simply wanted him to know he wasn't welcome around here. She said my scheme backfired which led to our father's death, and I can't argue with that."

Marco said, "But I can. No matter how you explain it, Stanton did the deed."

"But I pushed him to the edge."

"No, you gave him a way out, but he leaped into the chasm. You're feeling late remorse setting in."

"You're a psychiatrist now?"

"I wish I were. I'd know how to lift you out of this quagmire you've gotten yourself stuck in. You're not to blame. I might explain it this way: Stanton has a tragic flaw. It's called hubris. In his case, excessive pride coupled with greed was directed at you. He's the nemesis and you're the Goddess of Wine. His nature forced him to attempt to dethrone you."

"It's no use. I don't deserve someone as kind as you. I'm an evil person."

"You're not evil. What you did certainly wasn't evil. You were desperate to return to a normal life. Having a burden like that, you had to cast it off. You didn't shoot him or run him off the road or any of a hundred things you might have done. You simply wanted to show him he wasn't wanted, and tried a civilized way to do it."

"Marco, you are amazing."

"What?"

"After what I've done, and the way I've treated you these last few years, I'm surprised you want anything to do with me."

"I've never changed the way I feel about you."

"Then maybe it's time we settled a few matters of our own."

As quickly as it started, the weather outside settled down. The low air pressure had moved on and out toward the ocean. The quiet was peaceful.

The storm which had blown through the Valley earlier and settled down was akin to the tempest that had threatened Anna's very existence. With the atmospheric change came a feeling of peace and the confidence she could once again make good decisions.

"Was that a storm we just survived?" she asked.

Marco said, "It was a ruckus, meant to bring us to our senses."

"In that case, will you link with me in this pursuit of making the finest wine in the Valley?"

"Do you mean as a vineyard consultant, a salesman, a P.R. person—in what capacity?"

"No, someone much closer than any of those. Will you let me go by the name Preziano again?"

"If you're asking me what I think you're asking, I wouldn't have it any other way."

"You know we've never done anything to make our separation legal. I have not even changed the name on my driver's license."

"So we can annul the separation and live together without a court order?"

"Yes, we certainly can," Anna said. "We don't have to go through another marriage ceremony, but you will have to take me on a long vacation to relax after our ordeal. Call it a honeymoon or whatever. When we return, we can get on with creating that Premier Grand Cru fermentation."

"Yes, I definitely want that," Marco said, "but I think we should first have some kind of celebration. We could throw a little party where we could publicly announce our intentions, maybe a small-scale Roman Bacchanalia."

"Do you think that's necessary?"

"Hopefully it will help forge our renewed commitment."

"Will you show up this time?"

"Oh yes!"

She opened her arms for him. They held a long embrace which had her wondering why they had separated in the first place.

When they pulled away from each other, Anna said, "Let's make sure it works out for both of us this time."

Marco nodded his head, his usual method of agreement, yet he couldn't prevent harboring certain traces of doubt regarding her commitment to him. He thought for a while and then said, "The line from grape to wine threads from recorded history to the far-reaching future. I want to be part of that with you, if you will let me."

CPSIA information can be obtained at www.ICGtesting.com
Printed in the USA
BVOW081357231012

303702BV00001B/50/P

9 781936 154685